D0582200

RO⁻

Incident at Fall Creek

Charles Gilson looked for work when he needed money, and his line of work usually involved wanted dodgers and a sawn-off shotgun, so, on receiving news of an inheritance, he is determined to make a new start. But Gilson has competition for the money and Theodore Alden has charged his lawyer with securing it by fair means or foul.

With everyone, including Town Marshal Hardy, against Gilson, the odds seemed stacked against him, and it will take more than a few bullets to secure his future, and what is rightfully his.

Incident at Fall Creek

D.M. Harrison

A Black Horse Western

ROBERT HALE · LONDON

© D.M. Harrison 2014
First published in Great Britain 2014

ISBN 978-0-7198-1264-4

Robert Hale Limited
Clerkenwell House
Clerkenwell Green
London EC1R 0HT

www.halebooks.com

Typeset by
Derek Doyle & Associates, Shaw Heath
Printed and bound in Great Britain by
CPI Antony Rowe, Chippenham and Eastbourne

CHAPTER ONE

Charles Gilson spun the barrel of the .45 Colt so the hammer rested on an empty chamber. He'd only used one bullet. A young man was splayed across the saloon floor with his blood staining the sawdust. He had a neat hole in his chest; the argument was over.

No one approached the gunman. He looked round questioningly at the other customers but they backed away. He turned towards the bar.

'Another whiskey, barkeep,' he said.

He barely had enough time to finish his drink before the doors of the Lone Star Saloon banged open and the town marshal stood in the doorway with a loaded shotgun in his hands.

'What's happened here?' His question was directed towards the gunslinger but his glance scanned the whole room.

Gilson didn't attempt to touch his gun. His expression said he had a healthy respect for a man with a badge and a shotgun.

'The man picked an argument, Marshal,' he said. 'Ask

anyone here. He drew first.'

A few people nodded to confirm his words. The marshal looked at the dead man. His gun was in his hand. The gunslinger spoke the truth.

'Leave town now,' the marshal said. 'That was a young, stupid kid you killed. We don't want gun-happy critters here.'

'That kid became a man when he decided to tote a gun, Marshal.'

Gilson stepped over the body and made his way out of the saloon. In the silence that had shrouded the place since he'd shot the man, his spurs jingled and his leather chaps creaked as he walked across the wooden floor.

He reached his horse without any trouble. He reckoned the marshal was the type who wouldn't shoot a man in the back but probably wouldn't be too worried if someone else did just that.

Gilson had no particular destination. He looked for work when he needed money. His work involved wanted dodgers and a sawn-off shotgun. Unless he needed it he kept that weapon in a hostler hidden under his saddle-bags. The men he killed for the bounty didn't trouble him at all.

They had it coming. The young man's death upset him. He'd tried to avoid the fight in the bar but the youngster had been determined to prove himself a 'man'. People sniffed out gunslingers as if they had a particular smell, he thought. He watched people as they lowered their eyes to avoid him and decided that perhaps an odor of death hung about him.

He rode out of town and headed further west.

*

The clerk at Topeka Western Union looked up at the tall, dark-haired man, curiously. Gilson ignored him as he stared at the two letters, yellow with age. One looked so fragile he thought it might crumble into fragments.

'Those letters have come a long way to reach you. One's all the way from Indiana and the other one's been posted from around here and found its way back again.'

Gilson paused and looked up as if waiting for the clerk to tell him what was in the letters but the man started to stamp a pile of post.

It was only by chance the letters had found him. His ma had begged him to keep in contact and last time he wrote he'd told her he might head towards Kansas. And after the gunfight in the Lone Star Saloon he'd decided that it was as good a place as any.

Gilson turned the letters over and over in his hands for several minutes before he decided to get some coffee and grits and then read them. He smiled wryly; if asked, he'd admit he'd do anything to delay the task. He didn't like letters because they linked him with a past he wanted to forget.

Half an hour later at the Curly Dog Diner, situated off Main Street, he pushed his plate away. The meal was good – steak, potato pie, sweetcorn and biscuits to mop up the gravy. However, the big-city prices they charged, even at the shabby diner where he'd eaten his supper, left a sharp taste in the mouth. He drank enough coffee to float a boat down the Mississippi to get his money's worth. Finally, when he could delay it no longer, he opened the letter

7

that had travelled the furthest, 'from here and back again,' as the clerk said.

'Well, I'll be. . . .'

The letter came from his uncle, Bart Gilson.

Charles hadn't seen him since he was a little shaver. Bart was an uncle on his pa's side, who'd gone West twenty years before in 1870. The family had news of Uncle Bart from time to time – he was panning for gold, he was a scout with a wagon train, he was a fur trapper. Then, surprisingly, they heard he'd bought a ranch in Kansas in Wilson County, near Neodesha. Years later, when Charles was fifteen, Bart invited him to the ranch. Charles was in a lot of trouble at the time and never took up the offer.

The letter he now opened was a second invitation to the ranch. Bart explained that he wanted Charles to visit. He had a proposition to put to him that would be of interest to him. Also, according to Bart, the ranch was Charles's inheritance. Charles scratched his head; inheriting Uncle Bart's ranch was news. Inside were directions. The ranch sat near Fall Creek, several miles out of Neodesha. Charles shook the letter as if it would reveal some more secrets, but none came out so he put it down.

The ranch was left to him. Why him? Didn't Uncle Bart have any other living family? Rumor was, his uncle had taken up with a Mexican woman, and they had had a child.

He opened the other letter. The scrawling handwriting across the envelope had told him straightaway it was from his ma. Her script was a little shaky now but still readable. She explained that Uncle Bart had passed away. Charles stopped and checked the dates; Uncle Bart had been dead for six months. His ma didn't know the circumstances of his death; Jack Edwards, his uncle's foreman, had sent her the news. She'd also forwarded a separate letter that had arrived for him from Bart.

Charles turned the letter over and over. Bart had been dead for a while. What had happened to the place in that time?

He wasn't too upset about Uncle Bart, didn't know him well enough; but the letters left him stunned. It looked as if he stood to inherit a ranch.

'Well, I'll be. . . .' he said again.

He put the two letters securely inside his vest, which he wore under his jacket, and regretted that he might never know what Uncle Bart wanted to tell him.

Later, as he stood on the boardwalk outside one of the many three-story limestone buildings with their Victorian facades, he looked out towards the south bank of the Kansas River. In the busy street he pondered the question of what to do next. His virtually empty wallet decided his answer. Topeka was a big, expensive place and he was glad of an excuse to move on. At the age of twenty-four, Charles Gilson decided he was sick of killing and instead he'd go and claim his inheritance – the ranch in Wilson County, Kansas.

The leisurely journey would only take two or three days. In Charles's mind, there was no rush to get there. The Gilson Ranch wouldn't disappear overnight.

When he decided to go and investigate he didn't know what a can of worms he'd open up.

CHAPTER TWO

Lou Wainwright hit the scales at 230 lbs.

However, his feet left the floor when Theodore Alden gripped the collar of his shirt and pulled him out of the chair. His thin, wiry body belied his strength.

Alden owned a big cattle ranch in Kansas and he planned to increase his wealth.

'I paid you to sort things out, Lou,' Alden snarled.

Wainwright objected loudly. 'It's not my fault, Theo.' He began to choke as Alden's grip tightened.

'We gotta make sure about this land. You've got to try harder to find Bart Gilson's nephew, Charles. I want the Gilson Ranch.'

'So what you gonna do if I manage to produce him?'

The words came out in a hoarse whisper.

'I'm gonna kill him if he don't co-operate. So make sure he co-operates. You wouldn't want a death on your hands.'

Eventually, Alden let go of the collar and the other man fell back into the chair from where he'd been so unceremoniously removed. Wainwright huffed, puffed and croaked like a bullfrog. His suit now hung in creases about his large frame as if he'd slept in it. He eased his collar back around his neck and then pulled out a large handkerchief from his jacket pocket to mop his sweaty brow.

Alden crossed his spider-thin, black-wool-clad legs, his hands together as if in prayer, and waited. The two men sat opposite each other in the ranch house.

'It was a hot and uncomfortable journey here,' Wainwright complained. 'I can't help it if the news ain't good. You can't shoot the messenger.'

Alden ignored Wainwright's gripes. 'Look, it's been half a year and no one has made a claim on the Gilson's land. I reckon I can take it now.'

'America's a big country,' Wainwright said. 'I've tried to find his nephew with no luck, but there could be folks back East who are related to Bart Gilson. You got to be particular about dotting the i's and crossing the t's with regard to the land you want to claim.'

Alden considered himself to be a patient man but his patience was running out and he said so. He pointed his finger at Wainwright like a schoolmaster to his pupil. 'I'm telling you, Lou, by the end of this month my cattle are going to be running free on that land and those goddamn sheep of Gilson's are gonna be roasting on a bonfire.'

'You be careful, Theo: I hear the government's gonna start legislating about land speculators. Too many people have taken over land that doesn't belong to them. An' it's got a ranch house and outbuildings – you can't say it's unoccupied just 'cause the rightful owner ain't there.'

'By the time they get round to passing any legislature, Lou, I'll have the ranch under my belt. If you don't want to act for me, let me remind you that you ain't the only lawyer around here.'

'Actually, Theo, I *am* the only lawyer around here,' Wainwright said. 'Leastways, the only one that will act for you in this.' He moved back in the chair in case Alden took it into his head to heave him to his feet again.

'You let me know if anything crops up, Lou,' Alden said. 'I meant what I said – I'm gonna get that land if it's the last thing I do.'

Lou Wainwright arrived back in town to news of a stranger's visit. On further inquiry he found out the man's name was Gilson. He reckoned it could only be Bart's nephew. He paid a local boy to fetch Alden; he reckoned it was worth a couple of bucks to avoid being the messenger again.

CHAPTER THREE

Charles Gilson took in Neodesha, which sat between the Verdigras and Fall rivers where it had grown from an Indian trading post into a busy city. He patted his pinto paint horse's neck and soothed it as a new-fangled mechanical contraption rushed past them on the street.

'Things are changing,' he said. Steam billowed from the thing and it rattled and shook as the driver steered it along. 'An' I don't reckon it's for the best.'

He decided to aim for the nearest saloon to sup and drink and then find a bathhouse to freshen up before going to the ranch. He was on his second beer, an empty plate in front of him to attest to a good meal of meat and potato pie, when a stranger approached him. Although the man wasn't a young greenhorn seeking trouble, Gilson tensed and his hand hovered over his gun.

'Have a drink on me,' Alden introduced himself. Gilson nodded, but his manner was guarded. Alden snapped his fingers toward the barkeep and a bottle of whiskey, and two glasses, was produced.

Gilson reckoned the man wanted a hired gun so his

next words took him by surprise. 'Charles Gilson? I take it you're a relative of Bart Gilson?' he asked.

'I'm about to visit my uncle's place. Word gets round quickly in this town.'

Alden shrugged his shoulders.

'Even in a place as large as this, people notice when strangers come to town.' Then Alden frowned. 'I have to warn you, your uncle's place has gone to rack and ruin. I mean, Jack Edwards, Gilson's foreman, he's bled it dry, got a whole pile of money out of it. . . .'

Alden finished his whiskey and poured another. Gilson could see the veins along the side of the man's nose throbbing red as he consumed the alcohol.

'Another drink?'

Gilson put a hand across his glass and shook his head.

'No offense, but I've got a ride ahead of me,' he said.

Alden looked at Gilson's .45 Colt and his cartridge belt strapped low on his hips. 'None taken, although I'd have taken you for a hard-living man. It looks like you live by the gun.'

'You just tell me what addles you.' Two small spots on Gilson's cheeks went red with annoyance. He looked as if he didn't want the conversation to be about him.

The older man continued in the same vein, regardless. 'I could give you a chance to start afresh.'

'I make my own chances,' Gilson said. 'I don't want your help. I'm out to visit the ranch now.'

Alden's stick-thin frame leaned closer to Gilson. 'I think I've got a better proposition to put to you.' Gilson waited. 'You don't want to encumber yourself with a run-down place. It never prospered when Bart Gilson was alive, so it's a fairly barren desert now. All you got is a couple of sheep. And no one likes sheep here. They kill the ground. I'll give you ten cents on top of every dollar the place is worth, which isn't much, I can tell you. It's a good offer and you could buy a decent horse, saddle and some more guns and a rifle for the money. What d'ya say?'

Gilson finished what was left of his drink. 'Mr Alden, I thank you for the drink, and the offer. I can't say whether it's good or not. But whatever, I think I'll go and take a look-see and make my own judgment.'

Gilson made it plain to Alden he wanted to meet Jack Edwards – to find out if the man was old or just plain lazy to let the place fall apart He'd threaten that if he'd been living off Uncle Bart's money then he'd kick his ass from here to Pecos.

Gilson left the Longhorn Saloon. He was determined not to have someone make up his mind for him. He'd allowed that to happen as a youngster when his ma had packed him a few things and told him to flee after the shooting incident. It had been the wrong thing to do. Over time he'd worked out it was better to stay and face trouble rather than run away.

If he accepted Alden's offer he'd be doing it again.

He was wise enough to realize a man like Theodore Alden didn't walk up to strangers and offer them money unless there was a good reason.

Alden wanted the land.

Why? From what the man had said he already owned a large spread. Why did he want more?

CHAPTER FOUR

Anxious to see what would happen when Gilson and Alden met up, Wainwright made his way to the Longhorn Saloon.

He saw them deep in conversation so he got a shot of whiskey from the barkeep and then settled down in the corner to enjoy the show.

He could see the young man's irritation with Alden. Every so often a red spot would color his cheek and he'd bite his lip as if trying to keep his anger under control.

He smiled as he watched the young man finally leave. He chuckled quietly as Alden's face changed into something that would frighten the dogs off a gut wagon. It was good to see Alden not getting his own way for once. However, the pleasure was brief. Alden could make life miserable for a lot of people when he got upset.

The black mood grew darker as Alden turned round and looked at the lawyer. 'How come you never came over and joined us?'

Wainwright stood up. 'I didn't want to interrupt you. You were getting on fine until I reckon he didn't agree with something you said and walked out.'

Alden grimaced. 'You go and sort things out,' he snarled. 'That darn nephew of Bart Gilson's is determined to go over to the ranch. I offered him ten cents on the dollar over what he'd get anywhere else for it, but he turned his nose up.'

Wainwright did his imitation of a bullfrog and puffed out his cheeks again. 'That's good money. Might make him suspicious. Especially if he finds out no one else will make an offer over yours.'

'I reckon if his brains were dynamite he wouldn't have enough to blow his nose. Just find out what it'll take to make him leave.' He frowned. 'Or I'll take steps to make sure he goes.'

Lou Wainwright waddled out and saw Gilson unhitch his horse. He called out to him.

'Mr Charles Gilson?'

Gilson turned and saw a fat man approach along the boardwalk. His fingers touched the grip of his gun. It was a natural reaction but he didn't think he'd need his weapon. He looked down and nodded in reply to the question. The man couldn't match up to his six-foot-two frame, even with the help of the boardwalk.

'A lot of people seem to know about me.'

'The name's Lou Wainwright.' He pointed at the saddle on Gilson's horse. 'How come you put your name on it?'

Gilson frowned with annoyance. When his pa bought the saddle for him the fancy leatherwork seemed a good idea.

'Did you get the letter I sent?' A puzzled look came over Gilson's face. Wainwright wiped his brow. ''Fraid my bones

17

are getting too heavy to stand around for long,' he said. 'Do you mind if we discuss this in my office?'

Gilson didn't move. 'I didn't get no letter from you, mister. The letter I've got is from my Uncle Bart.'

'Ah,' Wainwright said. 'I was his lawyer. I can give you a lot more information.'

'I ain't got any money,' Gilson said.

'I don't want money. Your uncle paid me well enough to write his will, and to send a letter to you about it, which I know now you didn't get. So let me explain.' Wainwright pointed to a door a couple of yards away with a wooden sign hanging above it: 'Wainwright and Son'. 'Never got round to getting the "son" bit,' he said.

Curious, Gilson decided to follow the lawyer. The Gilson Ranch had been rudderless for a time so a couple more hours wouldn't make too much of a difference. He reckoned he might need as much information as he could get.

'Letters get lost, I suppose.'

The office wasn't much bigger than a cupboard filled with the lawyer's belongings. They covered a table and a couple of chairs. Piles of books in the window obscured the daylight. Wainwright lit the wick of a kerosene lamp to give them light.

'Sit down. Ah, wait.' Wainwright deftly collected a sheaf of papers with a sweep of his broad hand, then offered Gilson the seat. He did the same with his own chair. 'Can I read the letter you got?' he asked.

Gilson handed over the letter from Bart, which Wainwright skimmed, then immediately handed back. Although the lawyer sat surrounded by a chaotic disorder of papers and books, Gilson observed that the man knew where everything was. He immediately pulled out a small pile of papers bound together with a band.

'Your uncle came to me, mainly,' Wainwright admitted, ' 'cause there ain't no one else nearby.' He held his hand up to stop any comment. 'I try to stay fair, although it ain't always possible, but as I said, your uncle paid me to find you, and then show you the will.'

'You didn't find me. I told you I got my uncle's letter.'

'True. But I tried.' He held up the bundle and shook it before putting it down again. 'Anytime you want to read all these papers, go ahead; and there's a contract included that you ought to peruse carefully. However, I need a means of identification. Your uncle told me you could provide that.'

He sat forward and pressed the tips of his fingers of both hands together. Two red spots appeared in Gilson's cheeks again.

'I can see from your reaction that you know what I mean.'

'So why do you want me to say it?'

'A precaution.'

'Charles Wallace Leopold Augustine Gabriel Bartholomew Gilson.'

Wainwright kept his face straight as he handed over the documents. Gilson took the bundle but gave them no more than a cursory glance as he waited for Wainwright to continue.

'OK, I'll give you the bones of it. Bart Gilson made over the land, and everything that goes with it, to you. He has no other kin; he married a Mexican girl but she, and her child, died in childbirth. He told me he feels he owes you something. He asked me to warn you that Theodore Alden is after his land and that you'll have a fight on your hands.'

Gilson raised his eyebrows and grinned.

'I don't know anything about that. I do know that Alden's already approached me about buying me out,' Gilson said. 'He's got a big spread. Why does he want my uncle's place as well?'

'He just does, and that's reason enough,' Wainwright said. 'He wants to stop you carrying out your uncle's plans.'

Gilson looked puzzled. 'I don't know what his plans are, or were,' he said. He held up the papers Wainwright had given him. 'I suppose I'll find the reasons in here.'

'I can tell you, briefly, what they were. He planned to herd even more sheep. There's a whole bunch of them ready to come over from Mexico moment you give the word.'

'Me? More sheep?'

'Yes. The documents explain it all.'

'Don't sheep spoil the pastureland once they've been on it?'

Wainwright shook his head. 'Your uncle did a lot of research. He was that kind of man. Seems sheep will eat rougher grass than longhorns. His ranch land is a bit poor.'

'So it's sheep or nothing?' Wainwright nodded. 'If the land is so poor I can't make out why this Alden feller wants Uncle Bart's ranch. He's offered me ten cents on the dollar for it.'

Wainwright sat up from his slumped position. 'I've told you everything. I've done my job.' He pointed to the documents in Gilson's hand. 'I warn you, I work for Theodore Alden now and I can't advise you anymore.'

Gilson took the ribbon from the papers. A will. The deeds. A bill of sale for the sheep. A marriage contract.

'What's this?'

'You'd best ask at the ranch. It's quite complicated.'

Gilson shrugged.

'If you work for Alden why bother to give me this?'

'I told you, your uncle paid me. But now he's gone and Alden's paying.'

Gilson understood the man. Paid to do a job. Did it and then moved on. A lot like him.

CHAPTER FIVE

Gilson didn't leave town right away.

He bumped into the marshal as he left Lou Wainwright's office.

'I hope you're on your way outta town.'

Marshal Hardy, almost equal in height to Gilson, had a mean look about him and wasn't fancy with words. The marshal held a Colt revolving shotgun. It was a big gun with a barrel of thirty inches and its cylinder held four chambers of 10-gauge shot. Gilson didn't know this until the marshal told him. He sounded as if he wanted an excuse to use it.

'I don't like gunslingers hanging around.'

'I ain't here to cause trouble,' Gilson said. Although, from past experience, lawmen assumed that was exactly what he was about to do. 'I came to claim my inheritance.'

Marshal Hardy snickered. 'Inheritance? What you gonna inherit, boy? A vest full of lead?' He relaxed and lowered his shotgun.

'I'm Charles Gilson, Bart Gilson's nephew.' He handed

a letter to the marshal. 'This will prove I'm here on legitimate business.'

He looked at the letter. 'Oh, that's your inheritance? That's what you call a pile of woolly jumpers, is it? Lou Wainwright is the man you're after. If he's not filling his belly in Bell's Diner, he'll be drinking in the Longhorn Saloon.'

'Already seen him, Marshal,' Gilson said. 'He's got a copy of everything I got, just in case of an accident.'

The marshal raised his eyebrows. 'An accident?' he asked.

'Well,' Gilson said, 'I only arrived today and folks have taken more interest in me than even my ma ever did. So if you'll excuse me, I'm going to see the ranch now.'

Gilson left Neodesha Town and as directed he headed toward the south side of Fall River. The ride out to the ranch across Wilson County was pleasant on the eye. Definitely not the barren desert Alden had promised him.

'Plenty of grazing for you.' He slapped the neck of his distinctive pinto paint horse affectionately. Gilson could pick out his horse, with the dark star on its forehead, from miles away. The animal shook its dark mane that contrasted vividly with its white face, and snorted.

Gilson passed a couple of farms, all on the bank of the river, and saw cattle sheltered in the bottomlands. It looked as if there was plenty of timber available as well.

He forded the clear Fall River a couple of times until he reached the edge of his destination. The Gilson Ranch stood near Fall Creek, a tributary of Fall River that seemed to run along the side of the land Bart Gilson owned. On cursory inspection it seemed a splendid place and far from the wasteland he'd been led to expect. He reckoned he ought to take Jack Edwards by the hand and congratulate him. A fine place, he thought, so why had Alden only offered him ten cents on the dollar?

He frowned but as he neared the ranch he noticed that a large area of the land was shale. Perhaps Alden's offer wasn't such a poor proposition after all.

The man he took to be Jack Edwards didn't look too happy to see the newcomer. As Wainwright described, Edwards stood about five foot five with his heeled boots on, and had a ruddy complexion under hair turned white with age. The beard and moustache had yet to catch up, and was merely peppered gray.

Edwards, with three men behind him, stood at the end of the track that had led to the main ranch house. They were armed and Edwards had a shotgun to 'welcome' him. Gilson watched him slowly place two shells into the barrel.

'Just state your business. Then go.'

Gilson held his hands away from his gun-belt. He didn't want to provide the man with an excuse to shoot. He looked warily at the men who stood with Edwards. They seemed just as ready to discharge their weapons if given the word.

'Name's Charles Gilson. Bart Gilson was my uncle.'

Edwards' eyes reflected the distrust in his voice. 'Anyone could claim that. You got proof?'

'Got a letter in my pocket. Showed it to Lou Wainwright and he verified it as my uncle's will.'

Jack Edwards lowered his gun but the men at his side didn't. All three looked like mean grizzly bears to Charles Gilson.

24

'Don't trust Lou Wainwright any further than I could throw him. Last man who tried that broke his arms.' He smiled at his own joke. He thrust out his hand and demanded the letter. 'OK, let's see this 'ere paper.'

Gilson took out the letter. Carefully. 'I got Wainwright to make a copy. I have the original letter, and I left a copy with him. I told the marshal to look it over at his leisure.' He waited while Edwards scrutinized it. 'A rancher near here, Theodore Alden, seemed unhappy I'd come to Neodesha to make a claim,' he added. 'In fact, I get the impression I'm not welcome here by anyone.'

'Well, you could've stole this letter,' Edwards said. He looked as if the letter didn't mean much to him. 'Don't take a deal of brains to come up with a claim when all the county's been talking about it since Bart died.'

'Well, I got no more proof of who I am, than that.'

'Get down off that horse, nice and steady, so we can look at you. Bart was only four foot ten, so if you're tall I can count you out.'

'If that's so, then you've been working for an imposter,' Charles Gilson said. 'Ma told me Uncle Bart was that tall when he was born and he grew some more over the years. She said that my grandpa threatened to paint his feet black 'cause he couldn't keep up with the boots he outgrew. Don't remember him myself; he left long before I scrambled to my feet and looked round, but Ma and Pa told tales of the tricks he got up to.'

Again, a smile flashed across Jack Edwards' face but he kept it in check as he read the letter, word by word. Gilson stood by his horse until he'd finished. Finally he folded the letter and handed it back.

'Bart Gilson told me a sure way to test anyone who came claiming to be his nephew,' he said.

'And what's that?' Gilson asked. The look on his face said he knew. And he wasn't happy. 'That darn Uncle Bart. It was his fault I used to get into so many scrapes. He said to Ma it was like a document, but I could keep it in my head until I needed it.'

'Well, you need it now, 'cause if you don't recall your "document", I'm gonna blast you right back into town.'

Gilson heard three other gun barrels spin, ready to fire.

'My name. That's the document. I go by the name of Charles but my ma and pa christened me. . .' He swallowed before speaking again. 'At his suggestion my ma and pa called me after my pa, two grandpas and Uncle Bart. So, I'm Charles Wallace Leopold Augustine Gabriel Bartholomew Gilson.'

He screwed up his eyes so he didn't have to see the reaction of the four men. But he heard them.

'Charles Wallace Leo . . . what?'

'Never!' The men, now introduced as Ron Starkey, Floyd Barnes and Billy Kand, roared with laughter. 'Could've been worse – you could've been named after your aunts!'

Jack Edwards joined in the laughter.

'Oh, that's definitely Bart's nephew. No one else would remember, let alone admit to them unless under torture!'

'And what do we call you?' Kand asked.

'Chaz Gilson; that's the name I respond to.'

Gilson's hated list of names had caused the argument that had led him to leave town. Uncle Bart had meant well but it cost him a whole lot of trouble.

CHAPTER SIX

Invited into the ranch house, Gilson briefly scanned the main room.

It was basic, nothing too high-falutin', but the place sparkled and smelt of polish in a way you'd never expect from a home inhabited solely by men. The real woman's touch was a shining mahogany baby grand piano, given pride of place in the room.

'Never wanted to find another woman after his wife, Maria, died.' Edwards made the remark in answer to Gilson's unasked questions. 'There was a son but he followed his ma. Buried them together.'

The main room had several doors off it, one of which opened into a kitchen. The smell of fresh-baked biscuits and coffee filled the nostrils. An attractive woman stood next to the oven and stirred a pan of stew. She was, as Gilson found out, sassy.

She turned around and stared at him with dark-brown eyes. She smiled. 'So this is Uncle Bart's nephew?'

She wiped her hands on her white pinafore before she pushed strands of long brown hair back from her face and into a pale-pink lace snood.

Jack Edwards nodded. 'Seems like it. Got all the right documents.' Gilson ignored him and but heard the man suppress a snigger.

'The name is Chaz,' he said. 'You got the advantage on me, er, Miss. . . ?'

'I'm Señorita Juliena Halvillo. Your uncle arranged with my father for you to marry me. Part of the agreement is that he's sending over sheep as a dowry.'

Gilson stepped back and Edwards held his hands out as if to give support.

'I'm not ready to marry anyone. And, sorry if I offend, but if I allow more sheep here, you'll know I've gone loco! I'll negotiate my own deals. If anything I'd consider myself a cattleman.'

Juliena shook her head. 'It's not possible to change things. Arrangements have been made with my family and your family.' The conversation was over as far as Juliena was concerned. She turned her back on him and continued to stir the stew. 'Dinner ready in one hour. I bang the gong,' she called.

Stunned by the news, Gilson allowed Edwards to lead him away from the kitchen.

'I thought the lawyer gave you all the papers,' Edwards said.

'That don't mean I've read through them,' Gilson replied. 'This isn't what I want.' He looked back towards the kitchen door. 'I'm used to my own company.'

'You'd best see the rest of the place, son.' For a moment, Edwards lost his irritating grin and looked sympathetic. 'Help you consider what your actions might be.'

They rode over Bart Gilson's land. It didn't take long; it wasn't that big.

'You never said what happened to Uncle Bart.'

Edwards pursed his lips.

'He got dry-gulched. Juliena found him when she was out riding. It was too late to save him.'

'Did you find out who was responsible?' he asked.

'No. Marshal Hardy found no clues.'

They left the conversation like that. Over the ridge Gilson saw a sea of sheep like a passel of cream covering the land.

'When I first came into Greenwood and on through Wilson County I saw beautiful prairie grasses, trees, good grazing land, and yet my uncle seems to have missed out on a lot of that.' He pointed to a boarded-up contraption. 'What's that? It looks like a cross between a well and a mine.'

'Your uncle had the idea there might be oil on this land. He drilled and blasted but it didn't produce anything.'

Gilson frowned. 'Yeah, I saw bits of tarry stuff scattered around.'

Edwards continued to describe the set-up. 'It's not too bad on this stretch of land but it's not rich enough for longhorns. Don Halvillo offered Bart the sheep when he moved into the ranch with Maria. An' a couple of years ago the *señorita* arrived. Hence the offer of more sheep.'

'Ah yes, Halvillo. I think I'll ditch that idea. The sheep and the marriage ain't for me. I mean, she's attractive enough but I ain't come here for a wife. And if I ever get round to choosing one she'll be sweet, not bold and opinionated.'

'You don't ditch Don Halvillo,' Jack Edwards warned. 'He's well known here and in Mexico.'

'Why is he letting his daughter go to a stranger?'

'He and Bart go back a long way. When your uncle mentioned he'd got a nephew ... well, Halvillo's got six daughters, all married now except Juliena. It evidently seemed a good idea to match you up. An' he can get rid of her cheaply by giving the sheep as the dowry.'

Jack Edwards laughed at his own joke.

Gilson's frown indicated he didn't find the situation at all funny.

CHAPTER SEVEN

Alden stormed into Lou Wainwright's office as soon as Charles Gilson had left town.

'You brought him here,' he shouted. 'You and your goddamned interference.'

'It was Bart Gilson's letter that reached him. I never managed to contact him. I thought I owed him as much information as I had after Gilson commissioned me to write the will and such.'

'Principles are no use to me. Neither are you, because if I'd paid you first you'd never have bothered to find Gilson's nephew.'

Wainwright smiled and Alden snorted because he knew the answer to that question. Wainwright and money went together like a horse and cart or Gilson and sheep.

'Now, you find out as much as you can about him. Go through the wanted dodgers. Best thing that could happen is we find out he's on the run and we can get him sent to jail; or better – get him hung.'

'I could telegraph the place he used to live, Evansville, Indiana, otherwise I could be contacting all the towns he's ever been to. He's a drifter, and dang knows how many that could be.'

'OK, do that, and if anything comes to light, tell me immediately.'

The telegraph man, Fanon Tucker, at Evansville supplied Wainwright with a potted history on Charles Gilson. Tucker also happened to be the pa of the boy Gilson had had a fight with and left badly injured. It was the reason he'd left Evansville – to escape the consequences.

Most times the lawyer would've been pleased to find out such damming information but as he rode over to Alden's once again he felt out of tune with himself. Charles Gilson had seemed an affable enough young man. Then Wainwright recalled a photograph in the newspapers of another affable enough young man. William Bonney. That outlaw had a baby face.

'We certainly have him now.' Alden's grin spanned so wide he looked like a baked possum. 'As soon as he shows his face in town or those sheep come over the horizon, whichever is first, we'll drag him off to the marshal. If he crippled the kid then he ought to pay.' Alden looked pensive for a moment. 'Pity he didn't kill the critter. Would've done that boy a favor and made it easier to find a reason to hang Charles Gilson.'

'He wasn't convicted of anything, Theodore,' Wainwright said. 'He ran away after what was considered an accident. There are no wanted dodgers out for him. It was Garry Tucker's pa who gave me the story. He's got an axe to grind. I just passed on the information.'

Regret shaped Wainright's face and he looked weighed down with a load of sadness. The moment passed. He gave

Alden the bill for all his trouble.

'I'm going to have a word with Marshal Hardy,' Alden said.

It was agreed that Gilson would go into Neodesha with Edwards. They needed supplies and it was a good way to introduce Gilson to everyone. Juliena handed him a list of food she needed for cooking.

'I've sent word to my father,' she said. 'The sheep will be here soon.'

'You send another word,' Gilson said. 'Tell him to keep his sheep.'

Edwards laughed. He slapped his thigh and guffawed at the entertainment. 'You two go into town. You can get to know each other and then call in to make arrangements with the preacher.'

Juliena stood, arms akimbo. 'No way,' she said. She spoke to Edwards' disappearing frame.

'Looks as if you're stuck with me, Juliena,' Gilson said. 'I have no idea what to buy, even with your list. I promise I won't drag you to the preacher.'

She frowned but because she needed the items, she climbed up onto the buckboard and took the reins. Gilson climbed up after her.

'You OK with driving that wagon?' he asked.

For an answer, Juliena cried out and snapped the reins and the horse took off at a good pace. Gilson almost shot backwards and was forced to regain his seat on the buckboard. He looked at Juliena's face and had the feeling it wasn't going to be a very good day.

Gilson reckoned the journey into town was uneventful

if you didn't count the bumpy ride that nudged the two of them together or the fact that he had to avert his eyes from the outline of Juliena as the wheels caught every rut and made her sway seductively. The journey lasted several hours. They had no plans to do anything other than shop at the general store and get back before nightfall.

'Jack said you found my uncle's body,' Gilson said.

She turned towards him. Her brown eyes clouded with pain. 'Yes. He was a good man. Everyone liked him.'

'Someone didn't,' Gilson observed. 'The sheep weren't popular, either.'

'Alden stirred up those feelings.'

They lapsed into silence, each deep in their own thoughts.

They stopped at Brawn's general store and Gilson jumped off the buckboard and went round to help Juliena down. He gave her no chance to object and swept her down in one quick movement before she had time to argue. It didn't stop her from bawling him out.

'Mr Chaz Gilson,' she bridled, 'I can climb off a wagon without any help.'

'Maybe, Señorita Halvillo,' he agreed, 'but I don't see why you should deny me the pleasure of helping you.' Her waist was slim and his large hands almost spanned around it. Juliena shrugged and removed his hands from her body.

'I'm not here to give you pleasure,' she said.

'I thought you wanted to marry me?'

She colored and he grinned as she straightened her skirt and jacket. 'I have an errand to run first,' she said. 'I'll see you in the store in ten minutes.'

He watched as she walked. He noticed the way her skirt, divided into a pair of pants, hung seductively to show a well-shaped behind. He had no intention of getting married but it didn't stop him looking at a pretty woman. He didn't move from the spot until she'd disappeared into the next store.

Reluctantly, he turned his attention to his chores and saw that the horse had access to water and some oats in a bucket by its side. Then he leaned on the hitching rail and smoked a quirly. Fifteen minutes later he went inside.

The store was like any other he'd visited: shelves packed with food and household items. A basket of eggs stood on the counter together with jars of butter, barrels of flour, bags of potatoes. Meat hung from hooks – offal, ham, bacon, pigs' feet – mingled with flies. Spices, sugar, salt and pepper fought with peppermint and candles to produce the strongest smells.

Gilson saw the storekeeper holding the list. He merely stared at the paper. The fiery brunette, Señorita Juliena, tapped the floor with the toe of her tiny, booted foot.

'What do you mean you can't supply us? You supplied us last month, and the month before and all the other months. You been paid. What's wrong?' Juliena asked.

Gilson stepped up beside her. 'Anything I can help you with?'

For a moment it looked as if Juliena would refuse his offer. Then she said, 'Mr Brawn won't serve me.'

Gilson looked at the man. The storekeeper spoke directly to him.

'Folks is saying you're bringing more sheep to your ranch.'

'I ain't decided nothing,' Gilson said. 'But I don't aim to discuss my business here. All I want is for you to put this pretty lady's supplies on the counter an' I'll hump them onto the wagon.'

The storekeeper shook his head. 'No can do,' he said. He reached down and produced a wooden plaque from under the counter. 'Closed' was written on it in white paint. Brawn placed it in front of him. 'See what it says?'

Gilson reached over the counter with one hand, grabbed the man's shirt and lifted him several inches off the floor so they were nose to nose. He pulled out his Colt .45 with the other and held it to the man's ear.

'Let's not have a disagreement over this,' he suggested. 'You serve the young lady and I'll load it and we'll be off. Or I might get angry.'

Brawn nodded his head. They both knew it wasn't an argument he was likely to win by opposing a man with a gun.

They were halfway through the list when Marshal Hardy turned up.

CHAPTER EIGHT

The marshal held his Colt shotgun like it was an extension of his hand.

'Someone told me there's a disturbance going on here,' he said.

'Ain't no disturbance, Marshal.' Gilson looked around questioningly. The men who sat around the stove drinking coffee and chewing tobacco stayed quiet, their faces blank. Then one, more courageous than the others, stood up.

'The storekeeper is being forced to do what this sheepherder says.' He pointed to the gun, now replaced, in Gilson's holster. 'He drew a gun on him.'

'That true?' Marshal Hardy asked. His gaze didn't move from Gilson.

'What? That I'm a sheepherder or that I'm rushing the storekeeper to fill my order?' The marshal's rifle lifted up to Gilson's chest. 'I merely use my Colt Peacemaker to keep the peace.'

Marshal Hardy plainly disliked Gilson's manner. 'I've heard a few things about you today that don't sit right.'

'This town seems to have heard things I didn't know

about, either. Things I haven't even had time to consider,' Gilson replied. 'All I want to do is complete my order here and go back to the ranch.'

The marshal didn't seem to hear. 'I been told you shot a boy, left him for dead and ran out of town.'

There was a collective gasp of breath from the group of onlookers that had gathered round. A splash of tobacco juice hit the stove. Even Juliena, who'd stood close to him when the marshal came in, now stepped back.

'You heard half the story, Marshal,' Gilson said.

'I'll fill in the rest – the other half of the story is that the boy you shot is a cripple now. Can you tell me a convincing reason why I shouldn't arrest you?' Marshal Hardy asked.

'Arrest me?'

'Yes, 'cause I want to hear the whole story before you run away again.'

Gilson clenched and unclenched his hands. The man was calling him a coward in front of all the people in the store. There were women as well as men who might get shot if he went for his gun. He knew this and from the look on the marshal's face, he knew it too and was gambling that he'd come quietly and not risk a fight where innocent people could get hurt. The marshal's gun wasn't a weapon to be underestimated; it could do awful things to a body.

Gilson nodded. 'I'll come with you on condition that Señorita Halvillo's order is completed and placed in the wagon outside.' He turned to Brawn. 'Charge it to the Gilson Ranch as usual,' he said.

The marshal nodded at Brawn, giving him permission

for him to do just that, and Gilson handed over his gun and went to the jailhouse.

'I don't like your sort in my town,' Marshal Hardy said. 'Alden had information about you to give me. It made unpleasant listening.'

'You can't throw me out of town for something that happened years ago – an accident.'

'If it was accident why did you run? No, I'm gonna hold you here and get in touch with the marshal in Evansville.' Marshal Hardy pointed the shooter squarely at Gilson. 'Now, you get inside that cell. This shotgun is weighing my arms down. Don't make me empty it.'

Gilson shared the cell with a spider that looked at him suspiciously with all of its eight eyes. A couple of cock-roaches scurried across the floor.

'That's right, you practice good,' he said to the crea-tures, ' 'cause if I have to stay here much longer, I'll race the two of you against each other an' me and the spider will be placing bets on who wins.'

Gilson soon got bored, lay on the wood bunk, pulled his hat over his eyes and snoozed. He tried not to think too much. It churned up the brain and made things look darker than they were. It was difficult not to recall the past. Gilson reflected on his life. He'd never set out to be a gunslinger. A single incident had sent him along the wrong path.

The boy, Garry Tucker, was wounded and his folks feared he'd die. A silly argument that had changed two lives.

Charles Gilson had never used his full name, had no call to, but his friend had found out what it was and pranked around. Gilson was cleaning his gun, they'd got into a fight, and before he knew it the other boy was lying in a pool of blood. So he'd left home at fifteen, not knowing whether or not he'd killed someone. His ma encouraged him to run and somehow he never stopped running. She wrote later to say although Tucker was a cripple, the boy had survived and he ought to return. He never did.

A few months later he got into a fight and killed a man. His reputation as a gunfighter moved with him. One day, he knew, he'd meet a gunslinger a bit faster on the draw.

Home was a long way away now.

Gilson lived life as a loner. A hired gun. A bounty hunter. He'd thought things might pan out better for him when he got his Uncle Bart's letter, but here he was in another pile of trouble.

It was dawn when he heard the keys rattle in the cell lock. The sun's rays painted the cell pink and even the spider looked pretty.

'Got you some breakfast.'

Marshal Hardy handed Gilson a dish of stew through the bars that looked like leftovers made out of something that died last fall. Gilson accepted it.

'I ain't one to be fussy about food,' he said. 'Ask the hogs if they enjoyed their share of it as well.'

The marshal snarled at him. 'Prisoners are lucky to get anything that ain't been pissed on,' he said.

'I thought that was the reason steam was rising from it,' Gilson said.

He wouldn't let anyone rile him. It wasn't the place to be anything but civil. The food on the plate was hot and the coffee that came with it was hotter and it killed the taste. Gilson wolfed it down. If things turned bad then he'd need his strength to escape.

Gilson had to wait a couple of day in the jailhouse. Jack Edwards visited but said he couldn't do anything. 'Alden's got the marshal focused on getting an answer from Indiana.'

'It'll pan out all right,' Gilson said. 'I'll be at the ranch soon.'

He didn't feel that confident, though, and he thought he'd have to send for Wainwright soon. Maybe Alden was paying him, but Gilson reckoned that if he promised to pay him more then he'd defend him. Trouble was, he hadn't got a bean to bet on a cockroach, let alone pay a lawyer.

It didn't come to that. The marshal came in to see him. He looked disgruntled and irritated.

'Seems that friend of yours, the one you crippled, ain't made, or ain't willing to make, a charge against you. The man can't walk but it sounds to me like he got shot in the head.' Hardy opened the cell door, Gilson thought, with a lot of reluctance. 'Can't understand why I got such a quick reply. If it'd been me you'd've been rotting in here for a few months before I took the trouble to telegraph back. That's if I bothered at all. Tell you what, though, son, if your friend is forgiving, this town ain't. You got your supplies this time; next time find somewhere else to go.'

He held the door open for Gilson. He said nothing else but his attitude spoke volumes. Gilson moved quickly, picked up his Colt .45 and got out the jailhouse before the marshal changed his mind, locked him up again, and threw away the key.

He hadn't seen Juliena since the day in the store. He hadn't expected her to visit. Jail was no place for a lady.

At least, he thought, he wouldn't have to put up with her going on about jumping the broom; she might want to hit him with it, though. She was feisty enough to do that.

His mouth moved into a half-smile. It was about the only thing that had made him chuckle all week.

CHAPTER NINE

When Garry Tucker heard that there'd been an inquiry from the marshal in Neodesha it brought back all the angry feelings he'd stored up for years.

He and Charles Gilson had had a fight that changed their lives for ever.

'You got that water?'

He heard his ma's voice. He reacted automatically. 'I'm on my way,' he shouted.

He forced his mind back to the task of hauling water from the well. The contents of the buckets slopped over the edge as he walked towards the house. He carried them like a milkmaid with a wooden halter he'd made to fit over his shoulders. He had learned to be efficient at getting around with the aid of a tree branch fashioned into a crutch to go under his arm.

He blamed Gilson for his injury. He'd taunted him when he'd found out about his silly names. Unfortunately, the time he'd chosen was when Gilson was cleaning a gun. He couldn't remember the details except according to most folks they were hotheaded youths with little sense.

The thing he did recall was that he'd been left for dead.

The fact that Charles Gilson had rushed to the doc to get help didn't figure in the other boy's bitter attitude. He'd convinced himself that Gilson had run off, afraid to face the consequences.

It had been on his mind for years to search for him but he'd no idea where he'd gone. He wanted revenge for what had happened. He wished, on dark days, he'd never admitted it was pure accident the gun had been fired. Then Gilson would've been facing a long prison sentence.

When the pains shot through his knee like hot needles Tucker cursed out loud. He reckoned he could still feel the bullet rubbing inside, yet the doc said it had gone straight through.

'There you are, Ma,' he said.

He lifted off the wooden halter and plonked the bucket in the middle of the room. A tired woman bent over the washing tub, placed her red hands on her back and stretched, grimacing, as if to ease the aches in her body.

'It's no good to me there.' She pointed at the pot on the stove. 'Empty that into this washtub. Then put more cold water in it to boil. I need the washtub filled up.' She spoke slowly as if explaining things to a slow-minded child.

Tucker hated washdays. Twice a month the place stank of lye and dirty shirts, pants and sheets. He once said to his ma that he'd heard Indian women took their washing to the stream. He got a thick ear for that.

'Are you suggesting I act like a savage?' his ma had shouted at him. He didn't answer for fear he'd get the other ear matched to the one that throbbed. Nevertheless it seemed a good idea to him.

In the end he persuaded his pa to fashion a lean-to at the side of the house. Now they avoided sharing their meals with the washing although it didn't entirely take the unpleasantness away.

His ma forgot his injury and Tucker didn't remind her. It was difficult to lift the pot off the stove and carry the boiling water. The water splashed but he bit his lip as little blisters formed on his skin. He had grumbled once, but the pity in her eyes managed to say a whole lot more than any words.

Once, he'd hit his gammy leg in temper as the thing got in the way of him being a 'whole' man. He'd ended up writhing around the floor in pain. He blamed everyone for his disability instead of looking closer to home. Afterwards he tried to accept he was all boogered up until something happened to upset his carefully crafted exterior. Now Tucker dreamed once more about what he'd do to Gilson if he ever met up with him.

The massive power in his upper body made up for the weakness of his legs. Tucker's face, handsome without its scowl, attracted female attention. When young ladies first saw him they smiled and simpered. It became a malicious pleasure he enjoyed – to stand up to display the withered leg.

He wedged his weak side against the fireplace to give support and took the weight with his stronger side. Slowly, he lifted the pot and put it on the floor before he used his crutch again for support. He tipped it into the washtub and refilled the pot again with cold water.

'Thanks, son,' his ma said. 'Another two buckets of water should do it.'

She poured some extra lye in the water and threw in the under-drawers that he'd soiled when he'd been unable to get to the outside privy in time.

Embarrassed, he picked up the halter and went outside again.

Now he knew Gilson was at his uncle's ranch near Neodesha, he made up his mind to go and find him. He'd shatter Gilson's legs. He wanted him to know what it was like to be a cripple.

CHAPTER TEN

The stagecoach journey wasn't a pleasant one.

The wooden wheels bumped over every rut on the trail and the seats weren't particularly upholstered so they rattled and jarred all the passengers' bones in their bodies. There were four passengers, six people with the stagecoach driver and the shotgun rider.

If one woman hadn't timed the situation well, there might soon be seven.

'Can't this stagecoach go any faster?' Glenna Bonde's voice held both fear and anger.

A male passenger pushed his body through the opening of the window and shouted up to the driver.

'Need some more speed here, driver. We have a distressed lady on board.'

Stuart Narran barely turned his head towards the man, but he answered nonetheless.

'We're going as quick as these four horses can take us, mister. Can't go faster but I could go a hell of a lot slower if you keep disturbing me.'

Corrigan pulled back in and sat down. 'You'll be in

47

Neodesha soon,' he said. The tone of his voice didn't offer the same confidence as his words.

Glenna smiled. 'I'm so sorry to make a fuss,' she whispered. 'I didn't want everyone to know about my condition but this journey seems to be taking so long.'

A harsh laugh from the other woman in the stagecoach, Kitty Mattern: 'Missis, your secret was out as soon as we all saw you. Unless you're impersonating a buffalo!' Glenna Bonde crimsoned up with embarrassment but, chin up and resolute, sent a stony look toward the garishly dressed woman.

Kitty blushed and offered up a sort of apology. 'Don't worry, if you're took short. I'm a woman, and women are all the same, I'm told, so I'll help you. I'm Miss Mattern, by the way; pleased to meet you.'

She held out her hand but Glenna merely said, 'Mrs Bonde.'

Glenna shuddered but Kitty didn't notice. She looked at the man who'd tried to encourage the driver to a faster pace.

'Mr Neil Corrigan,' he said. He shuffled the cards he held in his hands again. He'd done this non-stop throughout the journey. 'If we have to stop I could distract the menfolk, Miss Mattern,' he said. 'Stop them worrying about what is really a natural function, beg your pardon, Mrs Bonde, and get them from under your feet.'

Kitty turned towards the other passenger, a quiet little man in the corner of the carriage.

'And you, are you a preacher or a doctor? Could you help out?'

Panic filled the man's eyes and he looked like a cornered animal. His face went puce. He'd not said a word

48

throughout the journey, except, when he had to, 'yes' or 'no' or 'excuse me'. The dark suit exposed what could be either a dog collar or just a tight-buttoned shirt at his neck. He clutched a solid leather carpetbag on his lap and didn't let go of it even when they stopped to eat.

'Take it easy,' Kitty said. 'Only a civil question.'

The man made an effort to control his emotions. 'I'm sorry,' he said. 'You merely caught me unawares. I'm not a doctor.'

Everyone looked expectantly, as if they were waiting for him to continue. Then Glenna doubled up with pain. Kitty moved and sat nearer the woman, placed a hand over hers and said ineffectual words like 'hush' and 'don't worry'.

The man continued his explanation of who he was. 'My name is Ruel Mead. I'm a lay preacher. I could say a prayer,' he offered.

'That's useful,' Kitty said. 'Well, there you have the total sum of the help we can offer you.' She looked at the gambler. 'I suggest you could shout at the driver to hurry up again!'

The comment produced a small amount of nervous laughter but it stopped as they heard a tearing, splintering noise under the carriage.

Outside, the stagecoach horses reared in terror and tried to get free. The whole incident happened in less than a minute but it had dire consequences for all of them.

Kitty seemingly woke up from a nightmare. She dreamed she was caught in a deep-blue sea that threatened to crush her with the weight of the water. She sat up and looked around. The nightmare was still there. The coach was tilted on its side. She and Glenna were entwined together and it was the woman's dark-blue dress that covered her. The force of the jolt had pitched Glenna forward. Gently, Kitty extricated herself from the wreckage. She covered Glenna up with a cloak and looked round to see how the others had fared.

Corrigan, his cards scattered over the carriage, grimaced as he helped the lay preacher back to his seat. 'Lucky I've got another pack,' he said.

Ruel Mead sat dazed with a bump on his forehead but his arms still clutched his bag.

'Those Bibles must be worth a lot,' Corrigan observed dryly.

'Hand-crafted,' the preacher said.

Kitty wasn't interested in the contents of the lay preacher's bag.

'Let's see what the damage is,' she said.

Corrigan climbed out first and helped Kitty out. He turned his head as her skirts kicked up to reveal red petticoats under her calf-length yellow silk skirt.

'That's rare,' she commented. 'A gentleman and a gambler.'

'A lady and a—'

'Don't finish that sentence,' Kitty said. 'Unless you want a black eye.'

'I was going to say a . . . Samaritan.'

'Humph,' Kitty replied.

They soon saw that the shotgun rider wouldn't be riding anywhere again. He'd been thrown off the stagecoach and fallen beneath one of the horses that'd kicked out as the accident happened. They moved Mo Wesley's body out of sight to spare the lady any more frights 'in her condition'. Narran put his hat on his chest for a moment as he acknowledged the man.

'Wesley and me, we been riding stagecoaches together for ten years,' he said. He put his hat on and continued philosophically, 'Looks like that dang stage company will have to find me a new partner.'

Narran examined the underneath of the coach.

'I told the company this coach was no good.' He shook his head. 'They never darn well listen, 'cause they ain't repaired it like they promised. I told them both those through braces needed replacing. I reckon they stuck it together with spit and paste.'

'No point in worrying about that now; we got a couple of people still in that carriage. Don't think anyone is seriously hurt, apart from your shotgun rider, so we'd best get them out.'

Glenna screamed as Kitty looked into the carriage and explained that the stagecoach had broken down and she'd have to climb out carefully to avoid any more movement.

'What about all the others?' Her concern would have been selfless if it hadn't been accompanied by sobs.

'Calm down, Mrs Bonde,' Kitty said. 'All this won't help the baby.'

When Kitty mentioned the baby it had the desired effect – at least it stopped the tears. Glenna blanched white at the gills and promptly threw up. Ruel Mead, who was sitting too near to her, got covered with the breakfast they'd consumed before they'd left the overnight stopover. All in all it was five miserable people who sat and discussed what to do next.

'How far is it to Neodesha?' Glenna asked.

'It's still a good half-day's ride away. Could take a whole lot longer by foot.'

'We can't walk,' Kitty said. 'Mrs Bonde is in too delicate a position to risk that.'

'What about the horses?' Corrigan asked.

'Not used to riders,' Narran said. 'Like as not they'd throw you off soon as you tried to mount 'em.'

'Has anyone got anything useful to suggest?' Kitty asked.

A lone rider on a beautiful paint horse rode into view. His gun, slung low on his hip and tied above the knee, sized him up as a gunslinger. Kitty picked up Wesley's shotgun. Narran had a Henry rifle in his hands and Corrigan slipped a derringer from his sleeve.

Charles Gilson, as he introduced himself to them, seemed oblivious to the weapons and asked if he could help. He didn't live too far away, certainly nearer than Neodesha, so they accepted. He quickly suggested they help Glenna Bonde out of the stagecoach by using Ruel Mead as a stepping stone. Gently, Gilson and Corrigan lifted her from the side of the carriage and deposited her safely with Kitty.

The rider, once they'd alighted from the carriage and were reassured that no one had suffered anything too bad, said he couldn't vouch for their reception when they got there.

'I thought you said it was your ranch?'

Kitty, never shy about speaking her mind, voiced the question.

'I've just inherited it. Everyone has to get used to each other. That's all.'

'But it's not too far away?' Narran asked.

'An hour, or two; it'll be slow going with, um, the lady.'

'You mean the lady with child?' Kitty said. 'Tell you what, we'll follow you. If your friends, or whatever you call them, are giving you a hard time, we'll pretend we've never met you before and we just happened along.'

'No need to do that, ma'am,' Gilson said. 'Just needed to warn you the reception might be poor.'

They made a stretcher with the stagecoach door and attached it to a pair of horses. Narran led the animals to make sure they didn't bolt and the others walked. Corrigan led the other horses, one with Wesley's body secured to it. All the passengers left their luggage, apart from the preacher, who still clutched his bag of Bibles. Kitty refused the offer from Gilson to ride with him and walked alongside Glenna.

He doffed his hat and headed off.

'Come on,' Corrigan said. 'Let's go after the man before he loses us.'

CHAPTER ELEVEN

Jack Edwards looked at the strangers with undisguised suspicion. He turned to Gilson.

'You know anything about this?' he asked.

Gilson nodded. 'I came across them when I was riding back here. They told me they were on their way from Coffeeville, Montgomery County, travelling to Neodesha.'

'Well, we can't accommodate them,' Edwards said. He had the look of a man who'd had too much happen lately. He lifted his hat, scratched his head and then replaced his hat again. 'Tell them to get on their way.'

He turned to go but Gilson put his hand out to stop him. Edwards looked offended. Gilson was aware he was putting a relationship at risk. He could make a bad enemy.

'I know you been in charge for a long time, and working on your own since my uncle's death, but things are gonna change here. You check things out with me first. Jack, I don't like the attitude of a man who don't welcome people in distress.'

Edwards frowned and then relaxed. 'Sure,' he said. 'I just had one hell of a shock you turning up, and then the trouble in town. Now this whole caboodle arrives. We ain't got much help around here; I had to let all but three men go.'

Gilson nodded. It was something of an apology. Probably all he was going to get.

'Thanks, Jack. I know it'll be a bit of trouble for you but these people are in a bad state. The lady on the stretcher,' he looked towards Glenna Bonde, 'she's in a particular way.' He coughed nervously, unable to say the words. 'I mean—'

'I can see what you mean,' Edwards cut in. 'We got no one to help out, unless she goes to Neodesha.'

'There's another lady, Miss Mattern, who said she'd stay with her.'

Edwards looked the woman up and down, immediately taking in the yellow satin dress, short on length and low at the front. He spoke softly.

'She's not a lady, Gilson,' he said. 'Don't think she'd want someone like that around her.'

Gilson grimaced. Then he said quietly, 'Jack, if you went to help a cow in distress with her calf, do you think she'd butt you 'cause you weren't wearing the right sort of hat?'

Edwards gave the words thought and then said, 'I suppose she wouldn't.'

'Can't Juliena help?'

Edwards shook his head. 'She's in her room packing. Say's she ain't gonna stay and wed a man who hurts boys.'

Gilson's irritation showed in his words. 'You know the story, Jack. How come she's waited this long to leave?'

'She just found out the marshal let you go.'

'I ain't got time for no hysterics. I'll go an' tell her what's happened.'

The expression on Juliena's face as she looked up from her task made Gilson hesitate.

'What are you doing in here?'

He knew she was right. Gilson had no business being in a lady's room, but another woman needed help. He didn't want her to leave with such bad feelings about him.

'I hear you're going back home to Mama and Papa?' he said. The words came out crueler than he intended but they were meant. 'You never struck me as someone who runs away from trouble.'

'And you never run away?'

She was right – he had run away.

'Left me with a lot of regrets.'

'Well, Mr Chaz Gilson, I'll have none.'

'There are people outside who need help. A woman's help.'

'I'm not staying with a man who hurts a young boy.'

'I was a boy as well when it happened, Juliena.'

She threw yet another dress in her valise. Her dark eyes sparkled and flashed like jet. He watched the way she flicked her hair from her face with her hand. He stared at the way she frowned. He looked as she wiped her brow and saw the perspiration run down between her breasts. He knew he didn't want her to leave. He took two steps and came face to face with her. A moment later she was in his arms and he was kissing her. She responded, her lips parting slightly before she pulled away breathlessly. Her next words seemed to belie the look on her face.

'Get out,' she said.

Gilson realized he'd overstepped the mark. He didn't protest. He left and closed the door behind him.

Jack Edwards sent Barnes with Narran to the stagecoach to see what needed to be done. They took the wagon to collect the passengers' luggage. A room was made over to Glenna and Kitty encouraged her to rest up. Juliena made coffee for everyone and soon the smell of biscuits baking, meat stewing and pots of potatoes and sweetcorn cooking over the fire permeated every corner of the room. Juliena strained the gravy from the meat and carried a bowl of broth on a tray to Glenna with coffee and cake for Kitty.

'I'm Juliena, and you?'

'I'm Kitty Mattern and she's Mrs Glenna Bonde.'

Glenna was asleep on the bed.

'Where's the husband?'

'Don't know. Didn't ask.'

Juliena put the tray on a table. 'Make sure she drinks all the broth. I know she won't feel like eating but tell her it's for the baby.'

Kitty took the bowl. 'You know something about babies, then?' she asked.

Juliena lowered her voice. 'My papa owns a huge sheep farm. I've helped at lambing time.'

'That's more than I know; however, I think the baby wants to come out and say hello real soon,' Kitty said. 'She's getting a few bad pains.'

'It's unlikely we'll get her into town, or get a doctor out here in time. We'll have to manage.' Juliena turned towards the bed when she heard the woman moan. 'How do you feel?'

The young woman asked for a doctor. 'The pains are so bad,' she said.

'There is no doctor. We will help you.'

Glenna Bonde wasn't reassured. She looked horrified. 'You're not even a nurse and she is—' The sentence ended in a screech as she looked out of wild eyes. Juliena patted the woman's hand.

'I've brought many little lambs into the world,' she said. 'And our friend here has helped other women.'

'You have? She has?'

'Yes,' Juliena said. Kitty bit her lip and said nothing. 'Now I will go and get clean cloths and lots of hot water.'

Juliena took Kitty aside. 'I'll come and look at her again. There is something for you on the tray, but will you join us for supper?'

Kitty shook her head. 'I don't think so.' Juliena turned to go but Kitty put her hand on her arm. 'You know, I'm not a lady like you. And I've no experience of this. . . .' She looked towards Glenna.

'We all have to pull together. Don't tell me you haven't helped another human being? Also it's not a time to make such distinctions. I don't. Or maybe you can't bear to be in the same room as me? I'm a Mexican.'

Juliena pulled her face into a pout and snapped her fingers and tapped her feet. 'Why, I might break into a flamenco dance at any moment!'

'I've come here for a new start.' Kitty looked towards Glenna, 'But already she looks at me as if I'm dirt. Probably all the others will, too. I was thrown out of the last town because the ladies wanted to clean up the place. They didn't like Main Street being known as The Red-Hot Street.'

Juliena looked at the woman, just past her youth, attractive but disheveled from the journey. Her clothes and hair were wrong.

'I'll introduce you as Miss Mattern. But I'll call you, Katherine,' Juliena said. 'Do you mind?'

'I like the sound of that name.'

'Brush your hair into a bun. Take those fripperies off your dress.'

Juliena had a way of taking over. Kitty had no argument with it. 'You can't hide the color of the dress, but tie this over your shoulders.'

She took a black shawl from a hook on the door.

Kitty nodded. The effect of the draped shawl muted her outfit.

'Thanks,' she said.

CHAPTER TWELVE

Juliena brushed past Gilson as she walked back into the kitchen.

She hadn't meant to but her mind was focused on other things. The two hadn't spoken since the scene in her room. They had pulled back as if a spark of lightning flashed between them.

Then Gilson asked, 'Is everything all right in there?'

'The woman Glenna Bonde is scared,' Juliena said.

'Have you got everything you need?'

Juliena smiled. She decided that what would, or wouldn't happen between them, had to take a back seat.

'Everything I need? I don't know. The luggage will be helpful. I'll need plenty of hot water.'

'I can haul water at least,' Gilson said.

The folks in the ranch were a badly assorted bunch but they were never meant to be together for long. Juliena introduced Kitty as Miss Katherine Mattern. Only Neil Corrigan showed surprise but didn't comment.

Juliena mixed enough dough to serve them all and more. She reckoned that at least there'd be plenty of bread and biscuits to satisfy the travelers' appetites.

The gambler sat quietly and played patience after failing to persuade anyone to join him in a game. The lay preacher refused to relax, as if it was a crime against the cloth, and sat on a hardback chair with his bag tightly in his hands.

It felt no cooler outside to Gilson as he stepped out for some fresh air. It showed in his face that he wasn't one for crowds. He surveyed the expanse of land that soon would be his and wondered if he was ready to settle down.

Jack Edwards brought two horses saddled and ready to ride. He nodded towards Gilson's horse.

'Took the liberty,' he said. 'Something's wrong with the water supply. It's coming in a trickle from the pump. We've got a trough full and that's all. The sheep need water as well as us.'

'Does that happen very often?'

Edwards shook his head. 'No, we got a good supply of water here from Fall Creek. In fact Theodore Alden reckoned he had rights to it because it runs along the border of the two ranches.' Edwards smiled broadly. 'Really upset him when Lou Wainwright had to agree with your uncle that the land deeds put it firmly out of his reach.'

'So how does he get his water supply?'

'Further across his range there's Fall Creek Lake. Not as good as Fall Creek, though. It dries up in a really hot summer.' Gilson squinted towards the yellow fireball in the sky. 'Almost lukewarm today,' he added.

Gilson smiled at Edwards' dismissive attitude.

The ride out towards Fall Creek was uneventful.

'Too quiet,' Edwards said. 'You can normally hear the river from here.'

The silence was shattered as a series of bullets pinged sharply off the rocks beside them. Gilson and Edwards dipped down low and used the sides of their horses as shields while they rode for cover.

'The ambush is ill-timed,' Edwards said. 'A while back they had the bulge on us.'

'Don't seem as it was meant to kill us. Maybe a warning,' Gilson said.

'Yeah, and look up there, see the creek ain't running down as fast as it ought.' Gilson looked to where Edwards pointed. 'The water is coming as slow as frozen molasses in January.'

'I think they've dammed it off.'

Edwards nodded in agreement. Then another bullet hit the rock by Gilson's shoulder and the pebbles flew around him, catching him in the face. He put his hand to his cheek and touched blood. He wiped it away.

'Just a scratch.'

Then a bullet landed by Edwards' boots. 'I think they're trying to get us to move,' he said.

'We'd best take heed,' Gilson agreed.

'We're not going to stay and try and fight?'

'We don't know how many we're fighting. We got guns but how much ammunition we got between us? We'll go back and decide what to do. When we're armed up we'll come back and blow them to smithereens!'

The people in the ranch didn't take the news well. Everyone was on edge, then Glenna Bonde screamed out from the back room.

'I'm lightin' a shuck for town,' Corrigan said. 'Too much trouble here.'

'It's that woman who needs to get to town,' Edwards commented.

'There's no way anyone will get to town in that stage-coach. According to the driver it needs major repairs. I don't reckon it can be fixed.'

'Anything can be fixed,' Narran interrupted. 'Needs a lot of work and it'll take a long time.'

Edwards butted in. 'Both through braces have broken and will have to be replaced.'

Juliena shook her head. 'Miss Mattern is of a mind that it won't be safe for Mrs Bonde to leave.' She nodded towards the door from which they could hear Glenna's distressing cries.

'I have to get to town,' the lay preacher grumbled. 'You must have a horse I could borrow?' Ruel Mead showed no charity towards Glenna Bonde's plight. 'If the lady can't go, then that's that, but it don't mean the rest of us can't move on.'

'Amen,' Narran commented.

Mead had the gall to blush but it didn't stop him. 'I have business in town,' he said. 'I don't have to stay.'

'What about your business here?' Juliena asked. 'The lady in there might need your prayers for her well-being.'

'God helps them who help themselves,' he answered. 'Anyway, who are you to give an opinion?' Mead's manner was terse. His gaze moved contemptuously over the young Mexican woman. 'When did we start listening to the advice of a whore and a Mex?'

Juliena stepped up him. 'Don't speak to me like that,' she said.

Gilson moved between them and threatened Mead. 'Careful,' he said, 'you'll be facing Dickens in a minute. I say preacher, or no, you have to look up to reach hell.'

Mead backed off but he mumbled as he did so. 'I suppose I know why you're protecting the Mex bit—'

He didn't finish the sentence. Gilson grabbed at Mead's shoulder, brought his arm back to give his fist extra force, and hit him. Mead lay on the floor out cold. Juliena's hand covered her mouth.

'I hope you aren't defending my "honor"?' she asked. She knelt by the man, her hand on his head. 'He's still alive. Let's put him on the sofa. Pull the side down and we can use it as a bed.'

Her instructions were directed at no one in particular but immediately they all came to help. Mead was moved to a more comfortable place than the floor.

'They said he suffered a bang on the head in the accident. Perhaps he acted out of character.' Corrigan offered an explanation for the man's behavior.

Juliena glared at Gilson. 'I don't think you can claim any excuses.'

He opened his mouth but she'd already turned away from him to tend to Ruel Mead.

Neil Corrigan continued to speak in an effort to break the tense atmosphere. 'Well, I think we've established that we can't move away from here yet. Let me thank you, from all of us, for your hospitality.' He touched his hat towards Juliena. 'The fact remains that we need water and that's what we ought to worry about.'

Gilson knew he was right and it irritated him to realize he'd been more interested in a woman than looking after all the people around him. He reckoned that if he wanted to make a go of it here, or anywhere, he had to put his own needs last. He'd lived alone too long.

'I think we'll agree it's decided. No one is going anywhere,' he said. No one disagreed. 'I need every man I can get.'

CHAPTER THIRTEEN

They heard riders approach the ranch house.

Gilson, with Edwards behind him, was about to step out when they heard Theodore Alden shout.

'Charles Gilson, I told you to take my offer and leave. I warned you. I'll up the price to twenty cents extra on the dollar. I give you that extra over whatever your uncle paid for this ranch. A man can't be fairer than that. You accept and you ride out richer than when you arrived. If not, you're deader than a can of corned beef. What'd you say?'

Gilson stood in the doorframe. His hands hovered over his Colt .45.

'You seem mighty frantic to own this land. Makes me want it as much as you do.'

Alden had a troop of twenty men surrounding him. He wasn't about to take a chance on being shot.

'Be it on your own head.' He told him he'd noticed the broken stagecoach on the way over. 'If you're sheltering anyone in there, then I'll warn all those people you've got inside. If they support you I'll take it they're against me.'

Juliena pushed past Edwards and stood by Gilson. She

looked at Theodore Alden.

'What's wrong with you? We've got a woman in there who can't move. Are you going to harm innocent people?'

'Out of respect for you, lady, I'll give everyone inside the ranch half an hour to start walking,' he said. He looked towards Gilson. 'I'll give you the same time to consider the offer.' Then he pulled at the horse's reins as he signaled to the men to follow, and then rode off.

In the ranch house Gilson explained to everyone what Alden had threatened. Edwards muttered, 'I don't trust Alden. Never have. I reckon he's got a lot of questions to answer about a lot of things. Trouble is, he's got the marshal in his pocket so nothing is gonna get done.' Gilson looked quizzically at Edwards but the man shook his head. 'It ain't the time to discuss things,' he said.

'So what's the plan?' Corrigan asked.

'I'm not sure I've got a plan yet. Any suggestions?' Gilson replied.

Kitty said she couldn't leave Glenna. Stuart Narran shook his head. His stagecoach was broken and he said he couldn't leave until it got fixed.

Neil Corrigan shuffled his cards as if they'd give him inspiration. He cut the pack and turned up the ace of spades. 'Don't look good for me whether I stay or go,' he said. 'So I might as well stay.'

'Looks as if we're all here to stay,' Juliena said.

Ron Starkey, Floyd Barnes and Billy Kand had moved onto the porch of the ranch house when they saw Alden and his men ride in. Although they'd confronted Bart Gilson's nephew, they were sensible enough to know you don't fight a bear with a hickory stick unless you're plumb mad or stupid. Now they stood inside ready to pitch in with everyone else.

Gilson looked around at the mixed bunch and decided he could count on the gambler, the stagecoach driver, Jack Edwards and three ranch-hands. The ladies had other things to divert them now.

Ruel Mead sat up, swayed and lay down again. 'I'm going to town. I don't care if it means a long walk.'

'Why are you so anxious to leave?' Kitty asked. Her hand touched his carpetbag and he yanked the bag so hard it caught on her sleeve. She pulled back, angry about the lace cuff turned into shreds, then looked dumbfounded along with everyone else as the bag came open and hundreds of greenback dollars spilt onto the floor.

'Don't you touch my money,' Mead shouted. He virtually rolled off the sofa and scrambled around on the floor like a beetle.

'I guess that explains his haste,' Corrigan laughed. 'He has to place all the church donations in the poor box!'

'Lay preacher! I don't think so,' Edwards said.

No one seemed surprised at the revelation that Ruel Mead was probably no more than a crook.

'You go if you want to,' Gilson said. He pointed to the money Mead was busily stuffing in his bag. 'That, however, stays here to be returned to where it belongs.'

'You can't do that,' Mead said.

Gilson pulled iron so fast no one saw his hand move. 'I can,' he said.

Mead stepped back. The movement was stiff and slow as

if it was part of his body he was leaving behind. Gilson nodded to Edwards. The carpetbag was scooped up and away before Mead had time to blink.

'Bart Gilson has a safe,' Edwards said. His eyes flickered towards the back of the room. 'I can place it in there.'

'Good idea,' Gilson agreed.

'I'll get it back,' Mead wailed. 'You won't get away with it!' For the moment the threat was empty.

'You're welcome to leave,' Gilson said. 'This isn't your fight.'

'I'm not leaving while you've got my money.'

'OK, stay, but I warn you that if you dupe us I'll make sure Theodore Alden knows about your stash.'

Mead chortled. 'He won't bother about me. He doesn't seem an honest man to me.'

'That's right. He'll have no qualms about taking it from you.'

The man shuddered and went back to a corner of the sofa, minus his bag, but still clutching his arms protectively around his body. With a quick, dismissive glance, it seemed Gilson set Mead from his mind and considered what to do next.

'I got this awful feeling that Theodore Alden will be happy to blast us all out of here to get this place.'

'It don't seem creditable that a man would murder all us folks just for a bit of land,' Corrigan said.

'He says he hates the idea of more sheep on the land,' Edwards said. 'He's been chuckling since Gilson got killed 'cause it meant no sheep.'

'I've heard men can get crazy about these things,' Narran said.

'What about the marshal?' Corrigan asked. 'Seems sensible to get word to him 'bout what's happening here.'

Jack Edwards' lips curled. 'Everyone knows Marshal Hardy is in league with Alden. He didn't investigate Bart Gilson's death. Reckoned it was a drifter who shot him.'

Juliena spoke softly to Gilson. 'I told you I found Bart. I handed over a bullet case, a Spencer .45, to Marshal Hardy but he said it weren't no help.'

'How you know that?'

Juliena looked with distaste at Gilson. 'I know how to shoot and I know guns.'

'Pity you don't still have the cases,' Gilson commented.

'Better than that. I got the doc to dig out the bullets. Not everyone is bad in Wilson County. They want to get rid of Theodore Alden.'

CHAPTER FOURTEEN

Theodore Alden had decided to act the moment he found out that Juliena Halvillo had been to the telegraph office.

She'd tried to send a message to her father. He had a finger in every pie or at least an ear in every building and the man at the telegraph office had warned him.

'That Mex is bound to have sent one of her men to her father as well. I reckon she don't trust a message that goes over wires.' Alden spoke as if he hadn't confirmed her distrust in the service. 'Don't bother to transmit it,' he ordered. 'I'll send a couple of my men to try and head off anyone who tries to reach Don Halvillo.'

The advice came too late; the message was on its way. The apprentice watched his boss toss the message into the wastebasket as she left the telegraph office and he retrieved the note. He liked Señorita Halvillo. He didn't mention the fact to Alden or his boss. It couldn't be undone.

*

It was at least a 600-mile ride to Halvillo Hacienda on the Nuevo León, but Milo Colbos knew this was important. Not only did the *señorita* want the sheep, she wanted her father to send men to help them in case of trouble from Theodore Alden. She feared the scale of Alden's fight to gain the ranch would increase now Gilson had arrived to claim the land. Colbos worked out it would take no more than two weeks to reach the *hacienda*, as long as he kept up a good pace, slept in the saddle and changed horses several times. It was a well-used route and he knew plenty of people at the outposts. His last horse had managed forty miles a day but it wasn't possible with every animal.

He knew some *amigos* reckoned the train was better. Colbos patted his horse's neck and reckoned nothing could be superior to the warm-blooded creature. People who hailed the advent of the iron horse would regret the passing of a wonderful means of transport, he thought.

Well into his journey a bullet flew past his head. A moment later another followed. The second bullet hit target. It was quick and sure and Colbos, minus his hat and the top of his head, fell forward in his saddle. The horse's front legs automatically lifted as the first bullet sprayed bits of grit into its path but then nothing else happened and it continued on its journey with the dead man on its back.

The shooters watched it gallop away.

'You think we ought to go after him?' Roland said. 'I mean, make sure he's dead?'

'Not many men gonna live long after their brains fall out,' Hill laughed.

'Don't know. Dodd's lived all his life with no brain!'

72

The three men were in a good mood. They'd done their job and got rid of the Mexican.

The *hacienda* consisted of a flat-roofed adobe house, a chapel, and beehive-shaped baking ovens, called *hornos*. The normally tranquil atmosphere had become chaotic, as preparations for a journey got under way.

After the telegraph from Juliena, Don Halvillo wanted to check out his daughter's husband-to-be. It would be a hazardous journey over to Kansas but they would use the Santa Fe trail. The number of sheep to be transported wasn't large; a couple of thousand ewes and a few rams.

Then he received news that caused some disquiet.

A couple of riders were heading towards the *hacienda*. A packhorse followed alongside them. The riders signaled peaceful intentions although people gathered at the gateway with rifles.

'They brought in Milo Colbos, or what's left of him. They found his horse wandering in the desert. They checked his coat and discovered a letter from your daughter, Juliena.'

'Give them hospitality and a reward.'

The Don sat in his study, with the door locked, and considered the letter his daughter had sent. He was concerned. He'd already received a telegraph from Juliena. She'd asked for help but he thought it was for the arrival of the sheep. It seemed help was needed more imminently than anticipated. She must've had doubts about the telegraph reaching him or why send Colbos?

He'd had doubts, constantly fueled by Doña Halvillo, about his daughter being so far from home. It had seemed like a good idea, that Juliena keep house for Bart Gilson. He'd known Gilson since he'd met the man many years ago. He'd been a visiting fur-trapper and proposed to his wife's close friend, Maria. The two had married with the family's blessing. When Gilson bought land in Kansas it turned out to be too poor, with its limestone and salt, for longhorns. He raised sheep like Halvillo.

When Halvillo travelled there with Juliena a couple of years back, she'd wanted to stay and a deal was struck. Bart had a nephew, Charles Gilson. Halvillo would supply more sheep as a dowry if the pair married.

'You'll need to convince me that they're suited before the final permission is granted,' he said. He made a joke but the laughter didn't reach his eyes.

His wife had been worried because her friend, Bart's wife, had died some time ago in childbirth, but the people seemed sincere about looking after his daughter. As far as he was concerned the prospect of marriage to the man's nephew with a dowry of ewes and a couple of rams had secured her safety. His wife had insisted he bring Juliena back home when Bart died but by then Juliena sent word that she wouldn't return. She was resolute the offer stood and she would wait for the nephew to arrive.

'Twelve months,' he said. 'Then you come home.'

That was six months ago. Now two messages had arrived at the *hacienda* – and one with a dead man.

The Don lingered for no more than it took him to organize the sheep round-up. He'd go with ten *hombres* and find out what was happening. Men, dogs and sheep would follow along the Santa Fe-Missouri trade route.

If all was well then he'd stay and see his daughter

married before he returned home. If he found trouble he'd bring his daughter home and the sheep would be sold.

Don Halvillo, satisfied he'd taken the right decision, went to put his wife's mind at rest.

CHAPTER FIFTEEN

'Is this a good idea, Alden?' Marshal Hardy asked.

Alden laughed. 'Don't concern yourself with what's right and wrong, unless I tell you to. I pay you plenty to do exactly that.'

The marshal colored up. No matter how much whiskey he drank, he knew what folks said behind his back.

Resignation replaced his initial anger. He'd never challenge Alden. He was in too deep. He had to keep drinking to keep out the sight of innocent men he'd hung on Alden's orders. As one of them said to him, 'You can shut your eyes, Marshal, but you can't shut your mind.'

'I'm only going to frighten him a bit,' Alden said. 'A few days in jail, trouble at the ranch, soon he'll reckon the whole thing's too much and he'll move on. I've seen his sort too often. Drifters with no backbone.'

'He's already had a spell in jail,' Marshal Hardy said. 'It didn't work then.'

'Well, this time you make it tougher for him. Jail ain't no picnic party.'

Alden turned away as if that was the end of the discussion on the subject. Alden decided he'd leave his men at the Gilson Ranch to take pot shots at anyone who stepped out the door.

'Fire frequent shots during the night. I don't want them to become too settled. I'll come back in the morning and see if he's ready to take my offer. I'm sure those other folks would've left by then.'

'And if he's not ready? Or those folks are still there?'

'I'll tell you what I'm about to tell Gilson. I'll shoot every one of his sheep, and then everyone who stays in that ranch house as well.'

Alden's threats were hard but to those who knew him, they were real. They'd butchered animals and men before on his say-so and would do again.

'What's gonna happen now?'

Theodore Alden's words had shocked them all. Gilson could still hear them echoing around his head. If he didn't leave then the rancher was going to shoot the sheep, and kill everyone who supported him.

'I wish my father were here,' Juliena stormed. 'He wouldn't take this treatment. He wouldn't let anyone kill his sheep.'

Her eyes blazed with anger and she stared at Gilson as if this was his fault.

'Right at this moment there are others to consider. If he's willing to kill sheep then how do we all fare in all this? His men are firing at everyone. They aren't asking our names first and whether we back Gilson,' Narran said.

'Yeah, I reckon that marshal is with him,' Kand added.

'So I can't see much use in going to town for help.'

'That man has always been in Alden's pay,' Starkey said. 'First time he's been so blatant about it.'

'Can't see why the feller is willing to go to all this trouble for a patch of land and a dislike of sheep,' Gilson said. 'Jack, you told me that Kansas had a fair number of sheep. I don't see why a couple of thousand more will make a difference.'

'You'll always get people who're stuck in the old ways. The days when the West was only for longhorn cattle are gone,' Edwards said. 'Times change and people are slow to adjust.'

'Some of my friends are still touring up and down the Mississippi on steamboats,' Corrigan added. 'I think it's gamblers playing against gamblers now!'

'That was close,' Juliena said.

She stepped back as the bullets blasted through the wooden shutters. From the bedroom they heard Glenna Bonde cry out.

'We need to restore water. We've got to act now,' Juliena warned.

Gilson's plans had been unresolved until Edwards said, 'There's a miner, not far from here, in Lock Skillet Gulch. My daddy said he'd blasted half of Lock Skillet. Cover us,' he looked at Barnes, 'and we could pick up some dynamite to move that dam.'

More shots broke up the discussion. One of the bullets ricocheted off the stone fireplace and came to rest against the opposite wall. The exchange of shots created the disturbance needed for Edwards and Barnes to slip out unnoticed.

'You'd best stay in the back room with Glenna Bonde,' Gilson said.

Juliena glared. 'I can shoot a gun as well as any man,' she said. 'I'll go in the room with them but take up a position by the window. They could've surrounded the building by now.'

Gilson nodded in agreement. 'I don't doubt your ability,' he said. 'Just forgetting myself and acting like a gentleman.'

'I'm sure you two can do your courting another time,' Ruel Mead said. Everyone had forgotten about him. 'I want a gun to protect myself.'

His gun, taken when the bag of money had been discovered, nettled him. He wasn't a prisoner but the consensus seemed to be that they were wary about the man and preferred him unarmed. But that was before bullets started to blast in.

'Give him back his gun,' Gilson said. 'If you make a move against us, you won't live to see your money again.' Mead nodded and Starkey went to hand his gun to him. 'Take all but one bullet out.' Gilson looked at Mead. 'Use it only to save yourself,' he said.

'That's worst than useless,' Mead said.

'No. One bullet to protect your own life. That way I'm not taking a risk. You can't shoot us all and make a run with your money.'

Ruel Mead looked at all the faces in the room. No one disagreed with Charles Gilson. He put the gun in his belt and sat down again.

Gilson checked that everyone had a gun that fired. Juliena had a Winchester repeater rifle, a present from her papa, she said.

'No one is going to get past me.'

Starkey and Narran covered the windows in the main room and Corrigan went to the kitchen to cover that side.

'Don't fire unless you can see who you're aiming at. They've got more ammo than us for sure,' Gilson said.

The men nodded.

Then Gilson checked on the women in the back room to make sure they were safe. He saw Glenna Bonde lying on the bed. Kitty sat by her side with a bowl of water and a cloth to the woman's brow.

'She OK?' He was nervous – he'd stepped into a territory no man liked to be in.

'Yes,' Kitty said. Then a moan broke from Glenna's lips and Gilson stepped back.

'Go away,' Juliena said. 'We're all right.'

She smiled and as she stood with the rifle in her hands, he felt confident that the women were as safe as they could be in this situation. He nodded and as another moan came from Glenna, he closed the door behind him.

CHAPTER SIXTEEN

Edwards and Barnes rode like the Devil was after them.

They only had eighteen miles to cover but they were aiming for mountainous territory. Edwards was out to find Ol' Pen, a miner as gnarled and old as the mountains, to supply what he needed. He'd found gold when he first arrived in Colorado but had lost it as quick.

'Why's he called Ol' Pen?' Barnes asked.

'Don't rightly know,' Edwards answered. 'Think he comes from Pennsylvania or somewhere. My pa said he purchased dynamite to blast the entire mountain to find his gold. As far as I know he's still blasting.'

Edwards hoped that Ol' Pen, who'd travelled with the first lot of gold miners, only then he was called Young Pen, still had enough of the stuff left to get rid of the dam in Fall Creek.

'You know,' Edwards said as they slowed down over some rough terrain, 'I reckon Bart Gilson's nephew might be just what the ranch and town needs. Someone who won't take too much from a bully like Theodore Alden.'

'Thought you weren't keen on him,' Barnes said.

'Not at first,' Edwards admitted. 'He took that spell in jail in his stride. He could've rode out when he first arrived, especially when Juliena looked him straight in the eye and told him she was going to marry him. He's stayed on to fight.'

'Yes,' Barnes agreed. 'But I heard he's a gunslinger. Fighting's in his blood.'

The pair rode on, each with their own thoughts, and didn't talk again until they reached Lock Skillet Gulch. The 'Keep Out Don't Trespus' signed by Ol' Pen gave them a location.

If men could be evaluated for their success by their clothes, Edwards reckoned Ol' Pen hadn't been successful. A man, garbed in overalls, a sombrero with the smell of oil to make it waterproof, and boots without a toe, appeared in front of them. He held a blunderbuss that looked as if it would inflict a fair bit of damage on the shooter as well the target and stood aiming the thing at them.

'Don't you come any further,' he shouted. 'Or else you'll be singing with the angels come supper time.'

His moustache and side whiskers were tinged with gray and a pair of bright-blue eyes set deep in a florid face, which spelt out drink, sun and age, stared out at them.

Edwards tugged on the horse's reins and held up his hand.

'Ol' Pen, it's me, Jack Edwards. My pa, Hone Edwards, used to mine the next claim to yours – weren't so lucky as you. Never struck more than enough to make a dollar coin.'

Ol' Pen squinted. 'Get off yer horse and leave yer gun

behind.' He looked out at Barnes. 'And you, whoever you are, stay back.'

Edwards gave Barnes the reins as he dismounted, left his rifle in the saddle holster, and walked over.

'Hold those hands high. Don't aim to have any stranger try to stake my claim.' Suspicion filled Ol' Pen's eyes. 'Yer don't look like your pa. Where is he now? I'd thought he'd come to visit with yer.'

'Been dead a few years,' Edwards said. 'When they made him they threw away the mould. Which is just as well 'cause Ma said she didn't want me turning out as irksome as him.'

'So what you want?' He raised the blunderbuss higher. 'Can't be here to socialize 'cause I ain't seen you before; your pa always left you in town with your ma.'

'If you'd seen me then you wouldn't recognize me now. I've grown up a bit and don't wear diapers no more.'

He waited to see if it would raise a smile. It did. Despite the initial hostility, Ol' Pen smiled and revealed a mouthful of missing teeth. He had only one upper and one lower tooth that clacked together as he talked.

'I heard you been blasting holes around here. I want some dynamite.' The smile vanished and Edwards paled as Ol' Pen's fingers tightened on the trigger. 'I mean I want to buy it from you,' he said.

'Where's the money?'

'I got plenty in my saddle-bag. Can't we do a deal? I'll pay you well.'

Ol' Pen wasn't open to the idea. 'Yeah, and soon as you get your "money" you'll pull a gun out your saddle-bag,' he said. 'No, siree. You ain't gonna take me for a fool.'

'Look, I'm not taking you for anything. If you've got dynamite, I've got money. We got to blast a dam that Theodore Alden's men made across our water supply. He's at the Gilson Ranch now, shooting at everyone, men and women, like pigs in a poke.'

Ol' Pen lowered his gun. 'Why didn't you say that first off?' he asked. 'I hear that man causes trouble for lots of folks.'

CHAPTER SEVENTEEN

Charles Gilson decided he wasn't going to wait for Alden's men to pick them off like fleas on a buffalo's back.

The shooting continued into the night.

'I reckon Alden's told his men to keep us penned in until he comes back to kill the sheep,' Narran said.

'Don't like sheep that much – bleating and milling around – however, killing animals like that is mean. I ain't gonna let him take what's rightly mine.'

Aided by a moonless night Gilson decided to make a foray outside. He picked up soot from the fire and smeared it across his face. Narran watched as Gilson went about his task.

'What's that about?'

'Learned a few things along the way that come in useful,' Gilson said. He smiled and the whiteness of his teeth clashed against his darkened skin.

'Keep your mouth shut and they won't see you coming,' Narran joked.

'Want some help?' Corrigan asked.

'You stay here. Return their fire but take care; the shadow flitting about might be me. Warn Juliena and the other two women that I'm outside.'

Corrigan nodded. 'I reckon that girl of yours knows how to handle a gun,' he said.

Gilson opened his mouth as if ready to deny Corrigan's comment but said nothing to refute it. 'Keep an eye on Ruel Mead. He's stepped over the line for the first time and God knows what he'll do next.'

The lights were doused to allow Gilson to slip silently through the doorway. He heard it click shut behind him.

He had his Colt .45 and a knife slipped into his belt. A shot rang out. Gilson froze. The bullet whizzed past several feet from where he stood. Then another. Inside the ranch they answered fire with fire. He kept his head down and hid behind a barrel. No one was aiming for him; they were shooting randomly. It was just as frightening, to be aware that a bullet would kill if it hit a target whether it was intended for you or not.

The flashes of light highlighted the shooters. A gunman was to the right of him and the other off centre. He waited, sheltered, and hoped for another round of bullets. He didn't have to wait long. Ten more shots rang out. He picked up none to the left so decided to edge around that way. He wanted to find out how many men Alden had left behind.

His feet were as light as a feather, barely skimming across the ground. The first man heard nothing as Gilson slit his throat. He had no time to raise the alarm as the warm blood spurted out and the residue trickled over

Gilson's hand. Gilson left him where he fell and continued to the next man. This feller was smarter and turned as if he'd sensed a presence. Gilson was quicker. He hadn't been on the run fearing he'd killed his friend without learning a few tricks. The knife came up and into the man's ribs, Gilson twisted the knife and it cut through the man's heart. Barely a gurgle escaped from his lips before life had been expunged.

'Kid, Jonny? You OK there?'

Gilson tensed. He knew Kid and Jonny were playing with the angels or more likely being tossed towards the Devil's imps, but their friend had no idea. Gilson waited. His breathing thundered in his own ears and he tried to take slower, shallower breaths.

'Kid? Jonny?'

Gilson saw the man approach, his eyes squinting to see in the darkness, and he beckoned him forward. The man noticed Kid or Jonny and said, 'You ain't shot one of those people from the ranch, have you? Mr Alden said only to keep them frightened 'til he returns.'

Then his eyes widened with surprise as he realized he wasn't talking to Kid or Jonny. He tried to pull iron, too late; Gilson's knife slipped in between his ribs and hit the centre of his heart. He fell; eyes wide open as he hit the ground.

The rest of the men were grouped to the right where most of the shooting had come from. An outbuilding, back of the corral, beyond the barn, sheltered them. Gilson saw twelve or more sitting round a campfire like it was a picnic. Another four sat nearer the ranch and took potshots at the wooden structure. He knew he couldn't go rushing in guns blazing in a situation like that because even if he could kill half a dozen it would still leave about the same number to fire back at him.

Now he knew the layout he decided to return. He, Corrigan, Narran, Starkey, and Kand would attack. However, it would leave the women exposed to danger because they'd have to fend off any strays around on their own. He thought of Juliena. If anyone could cope, she could.

Gilson slipped back into the ranch house.

'So how many's out there?' Corrigan asked.

'Three less than there were but that still leaves at least sixteen or so too many. I saw about twelve around the campfire. Another four shooters are out there as well.'

He outlined his plan to the men and to Juliena, who came to join them.

'You want me to come too?' she asked.

Gilson shook his head. 'Will you stay to protect everyone here?' he asked. His gaze took in the 'preacher'. He lowered his voice. 'Don't know what he's like to do. Mrs Bonde will need Miss Mattern soon, I guess.' A high-pitched groan from the back room confirmed his opinion.

'You've only got five men against them all,' she said.

'We've got the element of surprise and that'll make it easy to take out those slumbering around the fire.'

She placed her hand on his arm. 'Be careful,' she said.

He stroked her hand with his fingers, glanced at her, and fought a desire to take her in his arms. He pulled away abruptly but she merely smiled.

'*Cuidado, mi guapo amigo*,' she whispered.

CHAPTER EIGHTEEN

The idea was to creep up to the men outside the ranch.

'If Alden thought a couple of bullets would frighten anyone, then he's got it wrong,' Gilson said.

'It's like a mosquito biting on a hot summer day – eventually you'd have to slap it flat,' Starkey commented.

'You all got knives? I don't want anyone to use a gun yet. Save them for later.'

Corrigan nodded but Narran shook his head.

'I ain't no good at slicing things up,' he said. He picked up a poker from the fireplace. 'But I can sure bash their brains out.'

'Make sure you do it silently,' Gilson said. He looked at Kand.

'I got my lariat,' he said. He looped the rope and pulled.

'Give us a low whistle when the job's done. Otherwise keep quiet. I don't want anyone alerted before we surround them.'

'Five of us surround them?' Kand sounded skeptical.

'They won't know it's only five until we step out. If we

manage to creep up on them they won't know what's hit them.'

The other four gunmen Gilson had located earlier were quickly sought out. He sent Corrigan in one direction, Starkey and Narran in another. Gilson and Kand moved towards the two who stood together. They got close enough to hear them.

'I don't see why we can't go in and finish them off.'

'Boss wants to see whether Gilson will leave peacefully tomorrow. Somehow he's gonna get Bart Gilson's nephew to sign over the land for peanuts. At the moment he's playing games like a cat with a mouse. Keep up with the shooting,' he said. 'I got to go take a dump.'

Gilson watched him and then followed the man into the bushes. He waited for him to take his pants down and squat. He reckoned there wasn't any time a man was more vulnerable than when he was answering a call of nature. He stepped up behind him, a twig snapped, and the man turned. As he did so he got twisted in his pants and fell forward. Gilson followed and pushed a knife under the man's ribcage before he could utter a word. His bowels loosened in death so hc got to take his dump before he met his maker. Gilson reckoned he'd present one hell of a sight as he floated up.

Kand didn't need to get close to his foe.

'That you?' The other man looked round as something whistled through the air. His face registered surprised as a lariat wrapped around his neck. The rope, steel hard, fastened tightly and sliced through flesh.

Gilson heard a short, low whistle. He whistled back. Another one was down. Then came another whistle. And another. Four dead. The five men continued with their plan. They made their way to the camp.

'So how long we got to stay here?'

'Until Mr Theodore Alden has got what he wants.'

Someone spat in the fire and the tobacco-stained sputum hissed as it hit the flames.

'Could be here 'til doomsday 'cause that man wants everything.'

A general wave of laughter rippled through the crowd.

When Gilson slipped stealthily from an overturned barrel to the side of the outbuilding, he noticed someone give a fleeting look in his direction. Gilson froze, held his breath, almost as if it would make him invisible, but then the man shrugged as if the movement was a trick of the firelight. To his left Corrigan moved behind the men and to his right Narran got into position. He knew Kand and Starkey waited across from him. He fired into the air.

At this signal they all stepped forwards.

'Drop your guns,' he shouted.

Several of Alden's men ignored the warning and went for their weapons. Gilson and Narran shot them in the chest. It reduced the odds. Kand added to the confusion by using a larger lariat to lasso three of the men together and pull them to the ground. The others took Gilson's command seriously and unbuckled their gun-belts to let them fall to the floor. Gilson and Narran continued to cover them while Corrigan, Starkey and Kand roped them up.

'Have we got them all?' Corrigan asked.

'I think one slipped away just before we stepped in. He'll run to Alden. We'll be ready for him.'

*

'You won't get away with this, Charles Gilson.'

The angry words came from one of Alden's men as they marched them together towards the ranch house.

'No?' Gilson sounded as if he didn't believe in the possibility of defeat.

'Sure. Alden will be back in a couple of hours. The town is in debt to him. He'll bring more men. They'll be our friends and family and they won't like us roughed up by a sheepherder.'

Gilson replied to the man who had spoken. 'Well, I'll make sure those people appreciate your problems. I'll explain it's a good idea to leave the Gilson ranch alone.'

He looked at the motley bunch of prisoners. Many were shod like farmers in roughly woven clothes, or miners in overalls. The pile of weapons on the ground looked as if they'd spent most the time hanging on the wall rather than worn on the hip. The men were huddled at the base of a silver maple shade tree. No one was about to run away. The nooses round their necks, which had been swung over a branch, and hands tied behind their backs made sure of that.

Juliena's heels clicked across the porch. Her face was flushed. When Gilson saw her angry expression, he reckoned a mean rattlesnake would be proud to own her as its mother.

'I've known these men since I arrived here, Chaz Gilson. Met a few of their wives and daughters at church. You can't do this to them.'

92

'These men were shooting at us. On orders from Alden they'd have shot us all. I don't consider "these men" the type of friend I'd want to know even if we shared the same pew on Sundays.'

'You're as bad as they are,' Juliena continued. 'Barbaric behavior.' She turned and took a few steps, ready to storm back into the house, but she paused at the doorway. 'Can "these men" have any food?'

'Nope,' he said.

The door slammed.

CHAPTER NINETEEN

'Bothahrayshun!' Ol' Pen had run out of dynamite sticks.

'Never mind, I got a little blasting powder and that's as good as you'll need.'

Jack Edwards wasn't too sure about anything after listening to his tales of mishaps with jelly sticks. What damage could he do with powder? Seemingly ignorant of Edwards' doubts Ol' Pen rattled on about his exploits.

'Went deaf for a while in that ear,' he said. 'Think I stood too darn near to the explosion.' He banged the ear with the palm of his hand. 'All right now, though.' He smiled at the looks of horror on their faces as he explained how he nearly lost a finger. 'A piece of rock flew up in the air and it tried to scissor my nails off when it came back down.' His jolly face turned somber. 'I learned by my mistakes after Tom got blown up when I put a few sticks in the wrong place.'

He paused and watched Edwards' and Starkey's faces

blench and then he slapped his knee as he curled up laughing.

'Tom is my nickname for a jackrabbit that used to hop around hereabouts,' he joshed.

Ol' Pen insisted on going to the Gilson Ranch. He told them he was the only one who could use the powder. 'You might blow yourselves up.'

Edwards looked at Barnes with something of a resigned expression and shrugged his shoulders.

As they saddled their horses Barnes voiced his fears. 'I ought to be relieved it wasn't a man he blew up, but somehow I still don't feel good about it at all.'

'We need to get rid of that dam, so we have to let him come too. He's the one who'll carry it. Keep a safe distance and you'll be all right.' Edwards smiled but his face fixed into an unreadable expression.

The trip, however, was uneventful. Towards daybreak they reached the edge of the Gilson Ranch. They heard gunfire. Edwards made his mind up to investigate.

'A lot of activity down there,' he said. 'I'll find out what's happening. We'd best be careful. No sense getting killed.'

'Let's just go to the creek.' Ol' Pen volunteered his advice. 'We'll go ahead and blow the darn thing up, like your friend wanted.'

'Last time we got near the creek it had gunmen around it,' Edwards said. 'We don't want to risk being shot before we've planted the blasting powder. No, you stay here, Ol' Pen, and keep a watch out. Barnes will keep you company.'

'I'll stand guard over there.' Floyd Barnes shuffled nervously.

95

Edwards left his horse behind and cautiously edged his way towards the ranch where he'd heard gunfire and shouts. He couldn't make out what was happening in the poor, gray light.

CHAPTER TWENTY

A rip-rendering scream was heard from the ranch house. Everyone tensed.

'Thought you said everyone was accounted for?' Corrigan asked.

'Everyone I knew about. Damn, you don't think that runaway decided to play hero and turned back? He could've snuck into the ranch and hurt the women while we were busy.'

Gilson was already running as he spoke. He heard the sound of a slap and the screaming started in earnest. It came from the back room. He nearly kicked the door down as he burst into the room. A sight they hadn't expected to see greeted their eyes.

'Get out of here!' Juliena shouted. She held a baby in her arms and Kitty shielded Glenna from their sight.

'Beg your pardon, ma'am, er, miss, er, *señorita*,' Gilson said.

'Er . . . sorry . . . er,' Corrigan stammered.

The two men didn't turn; they walked backwards as they exited the room faster than they'd entered and

97

reclosed the door, gently.

Kitty tidied the bedsheets and made sure Glenna was comfortable, then Juliena handed the baby boy to its mother.

'Bit slow to start but he's fine and looking for a feed already.' The red-faced child opened its mouth, sucked air and screamed. 'Best get him suckled right away,' she said.

Kitty went and got a tray of food, as much for herself and Juliena as the new mother. Even in the chaos of gunfights and childbirth the women had coffee on the brew, a stew simmered on the stove, and a basket of bread stood near the fireplace. They got on with the everyday chores of life.

'I got something medicinal to add to the stewed coffee,' Kitty said. She reached into her travel bag and took out a flask. 'Best Irish whiskey this side of Kilkenny, so I've been told.'

Juliena smiled and took the drink. She coughed but took another sip.

'That-a-girl,' Kitty said. 'Not that I ought talk to you so familiar. I'm not in your league.'

'I'm from the same family as you,' Juliena said. Kitty looked perplexed. 'The human race. There's no one better than another. The only difference is some people make better of themselves than others.'

'That puts me at the bottom of the pile,' Kitty laughed. It was more of a sorrowful noise.

'You made the best of what you had. I thought you said you were travelling to start a new life?'

'Only 'cause the good women said they wanted a nicer town.'

'Take the opportunity they've given you,' Juliena said. She'd inherited her father's practical streak. 'You've already got yourself a new name – Katherine.'

Kitty pointed to her attire. 'This garb is all right for Kitty. Not Katherine.'

'I can give you a dress.'

Kitty was still unconvinced. 'And what do I do when I get there?'

'If I give you a dark dress you can be a widow woman in a town full of men looking for a wife.'

The rider whipped the horse into full gallop. The animal foamed from its mouth and its body was white with sweat. Along its sides the spurs had ripped into flesh.

Paul Dalloway fell off the creature and rushed into the Longhorn Saloon, where he knew Theodore Alden waited.

'He's dun gone and whupped us.'

Alden stared at the man as he panted for breath and flopped into a chair at his table. He raised his eyebrows as he signaled to the barkeep to bring a beer for the rider.

'Drink this and start again,' he said.

Dalloway downed the beer in one gulp and then Alden called for another. This one he sipped, then wiped his mouth with the back of his hand, and told everyone what had happened.

'Gilson and his men, must've been a dozen or more, killed our lookouts and then shot up the camp. I managed to put up a fight and escape but the others got caught.'

'I thought it was only Gilson, Edwards and his three hands up at the ranch,' Alden frowned.

'Must've been all those people who took shelter from the stagecoach. Don't know for sure but we were surrounded. Only just escaped with my life.'

Alden took in the shabbily attired man who hadn't got a mote of dust on him. He'd escaped, yes, but he hadn't put up any fight. Whatever the truth of the matter Alden reasoned that his plans had gone astray. He straightened his hat, patted his guns and called for the rest of his men to follow him. Lou Wainwright accompanied them. So did Marshal Hardy. He'd also left the ranch earlier with Alden.

'We'd best find out what's happened,' he said.

They rode hard until they came near the ranch. Then Alden halted.

'What's the plan, boss?'

'I can see some activity outside the ranch house. I think we ought to ride up and face it out.'

'So they can shoot us down?'

There were murmurs of assent but it was evident not everyone relished his idea.

'Got a better plan? Last time I left this place surrounded by shooters. I'm through playing games. I'll make the offer again and if he refuses, I'll shoot to kill.'

'That ain't legal, Theodore,' Lou Wainwright said.

Alden turned to the lawyer. 'Who's gonna say otherwise? Story will be that he pulled iron and it was self-defense.'

'I can't let you do that, Alden.' The dissent came from Marshal Hardy.

Theodore Alden laughed. 'You grown a backbone overnight?' He ignored Hardy and rode up to the Gilson Ranch with the look of a man full of confidence that he'd get what he wanted.

Gilson saw Alden and his men approach the ranch house.

'That's far enough,' Gilson said. 'Stop or I'll blast you out your saddles.'

Alden looked at Gilson, Corrigan, and Starkey. They had guns and looked ready to shoot.

'Just the three of you? You gonna take us all on? Come on, Gilson. I made you a good offer, which you chose to ignore.'

Gilson shouted, 'Get ready to fire.' The barrels of six guns poked through the shutters. 'Is that answer enough?'

Alden was unperturbed. 'I want you to free those poor men,' he said.

'And why should I do that?' Gilson asked.

'These good folk here ain't going to let you harm them.' He swept his arm round to indicate the assorted group around him.

'As soon as anyone makes a move against us I'll hang one of those men. And I'll keep doing it until you get out of here.'

'That's the extreme behavior of a lawless man,' Marshal Hardy challenged.

'And I suppose the threat to kill all my stock and every-one here should I fail to give up my land isn't the act of a lawless man?'

'If you do take my kind offer, it'll give you time to escape.'

'Escape? What am I suppose to be escaping from?'

'That boy you crippled. Seems his pa has encouraged him to lay charges against you, especially when I said there might be a reward. You'll be facing jail.'

Gilson blanched pale under his weather-beaten skin.

Alden's face filled with glee as he watched Gilson's reaction. 'Your past is catching up with you at last.'

'There's no reward on me.'

'There is now. A "concerned" citizen put a reward up.'

'No matter what, Alden,' Gilson said. 'It's my business, not yours, and I admit I ran away once, but I won't do the same again.'

Alden's smirk disappeared. 'Have it your way,' he said. He turned in his saddle and spoke to the men behind him. 'Right, you, you, and you, get to those sheep and start shooting.'

'I warned you, Alden, I'll hang these men one at a time. Starkey, put the first roped man on the horse.' He turned to the men round Alden. 'A word from me and he'll go to hell. Any of you know this feller?' He pointed to the first one in the line – the first one ready to die.

'That's Eustace Yannigan!'

'You can't hang him – he's got a couple of youngsters at home.'

Gilson looked unimpressed. 'Teach them a lesson in life,' he said. 'Being bad doesn't pay.'

No one moved. Then the man who had shouted out Yannigan's name threw his gun to the ground.

'I ain't letting him get hung over an argument about a few sheep.'

There were murmurs of agreement as weapons were dropped or stowed in gun-belts. A man's life is worth more than a sheep, seemed to be the general consensus. Alden said nothing. He looked down as if he knew the fight was over, at least for the moment.

CHAPTER
TWENTY-ONE

Inside the ranch house Juliena, Kitty, and Billy Kand had watched for Gilson's signal.

They had two guns each and thrust them through the gaps in the shutters. Gilson wanted to give the illusion of a greater number of people inside the ranch. Bart Gilson had kept a few shotguns at the ranch, all in good order and ready to fire.

Juliena saw the scene play out as she looked through the shutters. When she'd first met Chaz Gilson she'd taken him as a quitter. Not a bit like his Uncle Bart, who'd been friends with her father for years. It was a friendship that had lasted until his death the year before.

She recalled with affection her mother's fairy-tale story of Bart Gilson, the fur trapper who'd turned up at the *hacienda* to sell his wares. Instead he'd won the heart of her mother's best friend and companion, Maria Perez. Juliena came back to the present as the scene changed before her. She saw man after man behind Alden re-holster and put away their guns.

'Looks like your men aren't of the same mind as you, Alden,' Gilson said.

Theodore Alden's veins almost popped. 'What's the matter with you all? He wouldn't dare hang anyone. Take up your guns and shoot.'

'Will you let all those men go, Gilson?'

The question came from the first man who'd refused to fight and risk his friend's life.

'You can take the men and ride outta here. I've got no fight with you,' Gilson replied.

'What about all those sheep he's bringing over from Mexico?' Alden shouted. 'Don't you care that it'll ruin the land hereabouts?'

'You seen this land, Alden? Looks like he can't raise anything else but sheep on it.'

Laughter rippled through the group.

'Kansas is big enough to take both sheep and cattle.'

'Rob Derry has six thousand head of sheep. Sells it to those northerners who've got no taste.'

Gilson relaxed but not enough to take his guard down from Alden.

'I'll break any man who rides away from here without my say-so,' Alden threatened.

'How you gonna do that? A lot of us work for you but we can find other work. The question is, how will you manage if you got no cowpokes?'

Gilson saw Alden raise his Spencer rifle; he reacted quickly and blasted it from the man's hand. Alden screeched out in pain and grasped at his arm.

'Take my advice, Alden: turn around and leave,' Gilson

said. 'You ain't got any support now.' Then he looked at the men. 'I don't want a fight with anyone. Starkey, Corrigan, untie those men and let them go.'

'What about the men you killed? I got to arrest you for that,' Marshal Hardy said.

He'd sat quietly near Lou Wainwright but now, in the pay of Theodore Alden, the expression on his face said he reckoned he'd best speak up and try and keep his job. He was bright enough to realize that the changes happening would affect him.

'Those men deserved what they got. They were shooting at my friends and my property. Since when has this been a land where a man can't defend what belongs to him?'

There was a murmur of agreement about this, especially when Wainwright spoke up.

'He's got you there, Marshal Hardy. He's done nothing wrong. The boy he injured back in his home town hasn't made a complaint about him yet; he acted in self-defense when those four men got killed, and what's more, there ain't no law against keeping sheep.'

'Sounds like you're on his payroll,' Alden griped. He'd wound his neckerchief about his hand to stop the bleeding, his face crumpled and lined with the pain.

'I'm on the side of right here. You can't pay me enough to defend against wrong doing,' Wainwright said. He ignored the comments about being on the right side of who might pay him.

'Change of tune, I'd call it,' Alden countered.

Gilson refused to listen to their arguments.

'Discuss it another time,' he said. 'Follow those men's

examples and get outta here.'

'I'm still the marshal,' Hardy said. He had his hand on the Colt shotgun he carried in his saddle holster. Now he swung it out and aimed it towards the men. 'Anyone who leaves will get blasted. Pick up those guns and turn them towards Gilson.'

Gilson, although armed, hesitated. The gun Hardy favored would cause a bloodbath if he carried out his threat. The men picked up their guns, then looked at Hardy and then at Gilson. They seemed of a single mind; there was no question of what to do.

'Sorry, Hardy, we don't want this to turn into some kind of war.'

Their bullets riddled Marshal Hardy. He looked like a piece of raw meat as he sat momentarily on his horse before he toppled off. The marshal was dead and Theodore Alden had lost his support. The men were untied and about to leave. Gilson let out a sigh of relief as if he had a notion the worst was over.

Then came a God-almighty roar.

A sound shook the earth and the rain that followed the clap of thunder turned the ground, and everyone nearest Fall Creek, black.

CHAPTER TWENTY-TWO

Edwards and Barnes looked around as if in a bad dream. Ol' Pen wasn't anywhere to be seen.

'Thought you were watching him and the powder?'

'It's been a long ride, Jack. I only closed my eyes for a moment.'

Edwards shrugged his shoulders. There wasn't much he could say. He was all in, and had it not been for trying to work out what was happening down at the ranch house, he'd have been asleep as well. He scratched his head distractedly. It was a crazy world. Even Ol' Pen seemed sane after watching the shenanigans down there. At one time it seemed that Gilson had the upper hand and then he was letting men from Theodore Alden's gang go free. Edwards had no idea what to make of it. He turned round and went to discuss it with Barnes.

Meanwhile Ol' Pen did what he enjoyed most. He'd got fed up with all the waiting about and went to explore Fall Creek. He took his powder with him. The blockage was bigger than a beaver's dam and needed more than a couple of shovels to dig a trench through it. He reckoned a fair number of critters must've worked from dusk to dawn, over several days, to create the thing.

If it had been rock Ol' Pen would've had to drill several holes. Here it was a mixture of sticks, rocks and mud; and the resulting dam, although fairly solid, would've crumbled under the pressure of a drill. He used the skill honed from years of mining to size up the amount of black powder he'd have to use. He needed to keep the powder dry, so he took a few sticks of hollow bamboo and pushed them in. That done he put a long length of fuse into each hole, then poured the powder in and plugged a piece of lambs' wool in, to secure it. Ol' Pen reckoned on taking no chances.

He moved back and lit the fuses.

As the sound of the explosion rang in his ears, he realized he'd overestimated the amount of powder, but the dam was gone and the water flowed.

After the thunderous roar everyone at the ranch stood in silence. Spots of black tarry stuff speckled their clothes. Squabbles momentarily forgotten, everyone rushed to get onto their horses and rode towards the site of the blast. All apart from the injured Alden and Lou Wainwright, whose bulk gave him no incentive to rush anywhere.

At Fall Creek they stood and looked. They kept their feet well away from the black stuff that gushed about them.

'What happened?' Gilson asked.

Jack Edwards explained what he knew about it. 'My

man, Ol' Pen, decided to go ahead and blow the dam. This is what your uncle was looking for. It's called "black gold",' he said. 'Bart knew there was a reason, other than expanding the Alden ranch, that his neighbor wanted this land. He couldn't understand why the man couldn't see that it was useless for the grazing of cattle. He'd got a bargain, because the land was good for sheep, and no one realized he wanted it for that and was able to purchase it for a pittance. We had no trouble from Theodore Alden at first.' Edwards asked a rhetorical question: 'I mean, why would he want land that was barely good enough for sheep?'

According to Edwards, when the first sheep started to graze it produced no real reaction.

'People in and around Neodesha took things in their stride. It all changed when Alden rode from his ranch and took a short cut over the boss's land. His horse stumbled and he was thrown. He got covered in black "mud". Since then he plagued your uncle about the land and the water rights.'

Gilson stooped down and rubbed the black stuff between his fingers. Then he touched it with his tongue. He spat out the taste.

'Can't see why anyone would want this,' he said.

'The Indians knew about the stuff years ago,' Edwards said. 'They used it for medicine or sold it for lamp oil.'

'Yeah,' Gilson agreed. 'I'd heard kerosene could be got from crude oil, if this is what this is. I suppose if a large supply of oil could be found it could make a lot of money.'

People were quiet as the information sank in. Bart Gilson had been literally sitting on a gold mine.

Gilson and Edwards looked at each other – a question between them.

'How much did Theodore Alden want the land? Was it bad enough to kill Bart Gilson?'

CHAPTER TWENTY-THREE

'Looks like your plans have gone wrong,' Lou Wainwright said. 'Everyone has found out about the black gold.'

Alden trembled, his pallor white as blood dripped down his left wrist and onto the ground. 'No one gets the better of me. That Bart Gilson signed the paper to say I have equal rights to that water and the oil that's around there.'

'Theodore, that paper is as good as worthless. You forced him to sign—'

Alden interrupted him. 'You can't prove that,' he said.

'I can mention that Gilson died the same day you brought that document to me.'

'You got no proof I did anything wrong.'

Wainwright glanced at what was left of Hardy's body. 'No. Chief witness to Gilson's death can't own up to anything.'

Alden pulled a small derringer out of his boot.

'Don't do anything stupid, Theodore. I mean, how you

going to explain my death away? You can't have Hardy say
I was dry-gulched.'

Alden's lips pulled into a nasty grin and the two men
who'd known each other for years stared at each other.

'I'll think of something,' Alden said.

One man looked into the eyes of death and shuddered.
The other man's finger tightened on the trigger.

'Drop that gun, mister.'

Alden looked towards the voice, confident the shooter
wouldn't fire. A bullet winged his shoulder. He staggered
with the force of the bullet and tried to regain his balance
but fell to the ground.

Certain Alden was no threat, at least for the moment,
Juliena turned to Wainwright. The conversation between
Alden and Wainwright had confirmed her worse fears.
Bart Gilson had been murdered.

'I heard what you both said. I never believed a stranger
shot Bart. I've still got the bullets. If they can be matched
to any weapons he owns, I'll do everything I can to make
sure Theodore Alden hangs.'

'What on earth is going on?'

Kitty Mattern looked beyond the three people.

She had heard the ruckus and come outside. The dis-
traction gave Alden time to dive forward and try to wrest
the gun off Juliena. The gun went off and a bullet caught
his ankle. It stopped his flight and he howled with pain.

'Don't move another muscle or I'll shoot it. You'll end
up peppered with holes. The only reason you aren't dead
is because I want you to tell the judge all about Bart
Gilson.' Juliena's eyes flashed with the fury of her words.

At that moment a creature, which looked like a black

bear, came staggering into view.

Floyd Barnes followed, shouting at it.

'Shall I shoot it?' Kitty turned to grab a gun from inside the house.

'Let's wait,' Juliena cautioned. She squinted and shaded her eyes against the morning sun to see better. 'If it was dangerous there's enough men with guns out there. Somewhere. What you see isn't always true.'

She glanced at Alden as if he confirmed her words.

'An' I thought it might be dull around these parts,' Kitty laughed. 'I think I got to thank those prim ladies for booting me out.' She looked at Juliena and sobered at the expression on her face. 'Not that I ain't gonna make the most of the opportunity to reform. I'm just saying this beats any shindig I've been to!'

Juliena grinned. 'I agree. But I warn you it's not usually like this. Thankfully it's a little more er . . . sedate?'

'You gotta go and see what we've found, Señorita Juliena.' It was the excited voice of Barnes. 'I got orders to clean this man up but I'm darned if I know what to use.'

'If we had some water I could boil it up and give him a soak.'

Kitty stared at the vision before her. 'It's a man, you say? We thought that thing was a bear and debated whether to shoot it.'

'Don't you go doing that, ma'am.' The thing spoke up for itself. 'I'm dang well covered in gold. That's what it is. It's black gold.'

'You'll have water now,' Barnes explained. 'The blast was to get rid of the dam. Only Ol' Pen here, he put too much powder in the tubes and caused a hole the size of the Grand Canyon to appear. The black stuff has come from there.'

Gingerly, Juliena approached Ol' Pen. She reckoned he didn't seem so fearful once a name had been put to the thing. She touched his hand with her finger. 'You need to start washing down now. Take your clothes off. Get the stuff off your skin.'

If it was possible to see a blush under all the mess, Ol' Pen turned brilliant red. 'I'm sorry, ma'am. I ain't going to stand unshucked in front of ladies.'

'Do as you're told,' Juliena insisted. 'I'm going indoors to collect my magic lotion to help ease it off.' Ol' Pen nearly choked. 'Barnes can apply it.' She looked at Barnes. 'Take him round the side of the house. Avoid the corral and barn. Don't want to frighten the animals.'

Ol' Pen shuffled off, grumbling that he'd missed all the action.

'Haven't you seen enough action, old man?' his erstwhile companion asked.

CHAPTER TWENTY-FOUR

Kitty Mattern wasn't idle whilst Juliena organized the 'black bear's' clean-up.

She managed to get some rope and bind the wrists of the shot-up Theodore Alden. All the while he cursed her loudly. So loudly that the previously bed-bound Glenna Bonde hauled her body out of bed and to the door.

'You shouldn't be out of bed for another week or more,' Kitty said. She looked shocked by the pallor of the young woman.

Juliena was more philosophical and used to watching sheep with their lambs. 'No need to be bed-bound all the time,' she said.

Glenna smiled and her face pinked up with health. 'Thank you,' she said. 'I heard a real commotion and had to find out what was happening.'

There were moans and oaths, not really meant for a lady's ears, coming from the side of the ranch house. Kitty peeped around the corner and yelled, 'Boys, keep down the noise and button the language.' It went quiet as Ol' Pen's raw, pink body scurried from her view.

Juliena looked at Glenna. 'However, perhaps you've had enough excitement?' Glenna nodded and started to turn back. Then the unpleasant sight of Theodore Alden lying bound and injured on the ground stopped her in her tracks.

She fainted.

Juliena and Kitty managed to get the woman back to her bed.

'She needs some food inside her. She hasn't eaten properly for a couple of days and hunger won't help her to regain her health.'

Kitty agreed. 'I'll get a bowl of meat broth. That's a start.'

Juliena tucked the bedclothes around the woman and then brushed her hair from her face.

'You'll feel better soon,' Juliena said. 'Don't get up for a while without one of us around you.' Glenna nodded. She still looked dazed. 'Do you want your baby? It's been sleeping so long it must be near feeding time.'

Juliena smiled and turned towards the crib. Her smile faded and before she had time to utter a word, Ruel Mead stepped out from the shadows of the wardrobe, the child asleep over his shoulder.

He had a gun in his hand and pointed right at the baby's head. Glenna gasped but instinctively did and said nothing that might cause harm to her child. He glanced at Glenna. 'That's right, you keep quiet for your child's life.'

He spoke to Juliena. 'I have one bullet here; that's all he'd give me, that boyfriend of yours, but I'll use it on this little shaver if you don't do as I say. You know how to unlock that safe with my money. So do it,' Mead ordered.

Juliena walked in front of him into the main room. Right at the back by a dresser stood the old iron safe. She stealthily scanned the room. Kitty was somewhere in the house but she couldn't see her. She tried to stop her hands shaking as she opened the safe and took out the bag. She stood up and held it towards him.

'The baby?' she asked.

'Not until I get away from this place,' he said. 'I need a horse.'

'I'll get you one,' Juliena said. 'Promise me you'll let me have the baby then.'

She could see Kitty moving up behind Mead, her hand gripped round a rolling pin. An almost malevolent smile lit her face as she lifted her arm and smashed the wood over his head. He fell forward, let go of the baby, and Juliena caught the bundle before it hit the floor. Ruel Mead lay out cold and the women hardly dared to believe that they'd managed to save the little life that mewed in Juliena's arms.

'Let's get him back to his mother before he starts to squall.'

A moment later the baby sighed and suckled as it lay against Glenna's breast.

Kitty looked upset. 'This isn't right,' she said. She held a rolling pin smeared with blood. 'I had decided that "Katherine" suited me and I could take to the name. However, everything I do is more like "Kitty". Do you think I will ever shake it off?'

'If it hadn't been for you that scoundrel would've killed

117

the baby.' Juliena shuddered. 'You need a new start. Can you sew? Yes? Good, be a seamstress. Take some of this money to help set up.'

'I'd be no better than this man.'

Juliena would have none of it.

'You saved the child. A reward from heaven.' She took a quarter of the money from the carpetbag. 'This was never counted. Take it.' She looked down at Ruel Mead. 'There is probably a reward for him. However, it could take a while. You need it now. I'll make sure the money is returned later.'

Kitty laughed. 'God moves in mysterious ways.'

CHAPTER TWENTY-FIVE

Don Halvillo's caravan took a long time to travel to the Gilson Ranch in Kansas. His wife, and of course her entourage, had decided to accompany him.

Doña Halvillo gesticulated wildly with her fan as she explained that she was going, too. She was a diminutive five feet tall in her stockinged feet but the Don's large frame didn't daunt her. She placed her hands on broad hips.

'So where will you stay? There won't be room for everyone,' he said.

This claim didn't stand up as far as Doña Halvillo was concerned.

'The women will lodge at the ranch,' she said. She left unsaid the fact that the men would have to make their own arrangements. 'There is no way, Don Halvillo, no way, that my daughter is staying at that place any longer.'

Don Halvillo grimaced. His wife only used his title in private when she was determined to have her own way. She

119

continued without waiting for a comment from him.

'I will find her a good Mexican man. I have no time for your idea of an arranged marriage.'

She snapped her fan shut to underline the fact that no discussion was needed, wanted, or allowed.

That said it was agreed she'd go with him. He had to wait an extra half-day for his wife and her ladies to get ready. There was a frenzy of packing, enough baggage for a year, rather than the two weeks he planned on. He reckoned that would be enough time to collect his daughter and make sure that Bart Gilson's nephew had no claim on her.

He'd liked Bart. He'd known him first when, as a youth, he'd turned up at the *hacienda* to sell skins and trinkets, none of which they wanted or needed, but he charmed the ladies and was invited to stay for dinner.

Don Halvillo now made his fourth journey from Mexico to Kansas, and as the caravan of people rolled along, and his joints ached with age, he hoped this would be the last time. He decided he was too old for long journeys.

Eventually, in the distance, he could see the ranch. Somehow it didn't look the same although he couldn't put his finger on the change. The land looked rough and uninviting and he wondered if it was even suitable for sheep. Yet the land had salt and water and he knew Bart had supplemented the poor grazing with grain and grass hay. As he got nearer he saw the ground blackened in parts. He squinted to try to see clearly but couldn't make out what it was. The sight dismayed his wife.

'What has happened? Oh, my poor girl!'

Doña Halvillo fluttered her eyelashes. The fan vibrated

with each word as if it had its own existence.

Don Halvillo signaled to four of the men to follow and told the rest to remain with the women and the carriages.

'Stay here,' he said. 'I'll investigate.'

Doña Halvillo again voiced her objections. She informed him she had other plans.

'Don Halvillo, you expect me to hold back when my daughter could be at risk?' For a large lady she nimbly dismounted the carriage and ordered one of the Don's men to help her onto a horse. 'I'm coming with you,' she said.

Although strong in many ways, Halvillo usually lost a fight with his wife. This time was no different.

CHAPTER TWENTY-SIX

Juliena's dark-blue dress swept over the foot of the rocker and onto the porch floor as she pushed the chair backwards and forwards with the toe of her shoe in a gentle rhythm.

The baby lay in her arms sleeping after its feed to allow its mother some rest. Glenna Bonde had a lot to recover from: the death of her husband, the birth, and worse – the knowledge that the uncle she had come to ask for help was a crook and possibly a murderer.

Glenna told Juliena and Kitty that she and her husband had moved West to find a better life. Things hadn't gone to plan. Her husband hadn't been involved in a fight, but a stray bullet had killed him as he walked along the boardwalk. She'd had no female relatives to turn to and decided to seek out her Uncle Ally who lived near Neodesha.

The relative turned out to be Theodore Alden.

Glenna wept inconsolably at times but the women agreed it was something that happened after birth and treated it as a natural thing.

'We'll sort something out,' Juliena said.

It had certainly been a hectic time, one that had left her glad of this short respite. Truth was, as she rocked the baby, she had no idea what to do. Eventually, her eyelids drooped and she nodded off. It was the sleep of a cat ready to wake to any movement or sound.

'She looks pretty as a picture, especially with the babe in her arms.'

It was Gilson who spoke. Juliena's eyes stayed closed as she listened to the conversation.

'Do you think you will get married?'

It was Jack Edwards' voice.

'Don't reckon I stand a chance. Judging by her reactions I think I'm as attractive to her as a dime's worth of dog meat. Anyways, I got a lot of past to explain.'

Juliena wondered if he was referring to the young friend he'd maimed. She'd been taken aback at that information, but she supposed it was as easy to do that as to shoot someone dead.

'There aren't many men in the West who don't come with a lot of baggage. Your fight is in the past and here is the place for a fresh start.'

'I suppose so.' Gilson's voice didn't hold much conviction. However, from his next comment it seemed to Juliena that his mind was on other things. 'Do you think Wainwright will be any help to us?' Gilson asked.

'Wainwright's proved a good advisor in the past – that is if you paid him well. You can trust him if you hold the purse,' Edwards advised. 'He said he could get in touch with a Mr McDermott. Some expert who'll come over and judge how much oil you got.'

'I'd just like to burn it off,' Gilson said.

Edwards didn't agree. 'It'd burn for ever if there's a lot underground. And what's the sense in that? You'll make enough money; sheep won't matter a baa anymore.'

Edwards laughed at his own joke but Gilson had the last word.

'All I can see is a black, oily mess over the land.'

The conversation stopped and Juliena resisted opening her eyes. She wanted to sink back into sleep. However, it wasn't to be.

'There's a group of people riding hell for leather towards us,' Edwards said. He shaded his eyes with his hands. 'Can't see who they are – damn sun is right in my eyes.'

'Call Starkey, Barnes, and Kand and we'll put up a show,' Gilson said. 'Pity Corrigan had to leave to take Ruel Mead into town.'

'After what Mead tried to do?' Edwards remarked. 'Jail is the best place for that fellow.'

Juliena did react to that. If there was any danger she had to take the baby inside and get a gun. She stood up abruptly, glanced at the men and then went into the house.

Inside the ranch Kitty was chopping the vegetables for supper.

'Leave that,' Juliena said. 'We got riders coming in.' Kitty nodded. 'Go to Glenna's side.'

Juliena handed her the baby before she picked up a shotgun, broke it open to insert a couple of slugs, and then snapped it back together.

The dust enveloped them as they rode along the winding trail to the ranch. Don Halvillo didn't anticipate a shoot-out. He didn't think it would come to that but he was prepared to fight if necessary.

His wife was unarmed. It was something he'd debated the necessity of for a long time. It seemed, though, however many times she had shooting lessons it made no difference to her skills. She was abysmal and more of a danger to herself than others. All his daughters were wonderful marksmen. They took after him with this skill, and thankfully, not after their mother.

It was one of those daughters who now aimed a shotgun at him. He saw Jack Edwards at her side and Floyd Barnes and Ron Starkey stepping up. He didn't know the fellow at the front of the group but presumed it was Bart's nephew. He was shaken at how much he looked like the hunter frontiersman who had won Maria Perez's heart. He had the same ice-blue eyes and stared in the same manner as his uncle had when he first came to the *hacienda*.

'That's close enough, mister,' the young man said. 'We don't like strangers coming up to the Gilson Ranch without properly introducing themselves. Keep those hands above your gun-belt so we can see you all ain't gonna draw on us.'

Everyone acted cautiously. No one wanted a movement misinterpreted. Doña Halvillo had no such qualms and moved her horse forward. Her voice boomed out into the silence.

'Do I look as if I'm going to draw on you, young man?'

Edwards blinked once, twice.

'Doña Halvillo?'

Juliena stepped out onto the porch.

'Mama? Papa?'

Inside the ranch house a baby cried loudly.

'I think, Don Halvillo, we'd best sort out what has happened here,' his wife said. 'Although it sounds as if we're too late.'

CHAPTER TWENTY-SEVEN

Kitty remained inside the ranch house with the baby and its mother.

When she'd heard the woman outside was Juliena's mother, who she surmised was a formidable foe, she was thankful she'd been persuaded by Juliena to shed the personality of 'Kitty'.

She stepped up to the bowl on the dresser, pausing only to wash her hands and face, before she checked her hair. Attired in the dark-brown dress Juliena had given to her, 'Kitty' had gone and only 'Katherine' remained. The image of a respectable widow reflected back at her.

She'd disposed of the yellow and red taffeta garb by making it into a quilt for the baby. Glenna and Katherine had become close friends. A friendship developed through adversity. They were both alone and needed support to start a new life. Glenna's dream of living with her uncle had been shattered.

Theodore Alden languished in jail with his tail between

his legs and plenty of bandages on his body. Everyone agreed that Bart Gilson's death had to be investigated.

Wainwright said Glenna Bonde could stay at a hotel in town while things were arranged, as she stood to inherit the ranch if Alden hanged. The look on her face, however, made it plain she had no intention of setting foot on his land. Wainwright explained she was entitled to the money from the sale of the ranch. She had to consider what was best for her son.

Katherine was ready to receive Doña Halvillo when she strode into the room without knocking. She'd positioned herself demurely on a chair next to Glenna, who held the baby in her arms. She looked up with feigned surprise and stood up immediately.

'Can I help you? I'm Mrs Katherine Mattern. Mrs Glenna Bonde isn't taking visitors at the moment, I'm afraid.'

It was the last thing the Doña expected. In fact she didn't know, other than the worse, what to expect. Her puffed-up indignation deflated as she took in the scene.

'*Por favor*,' she exclaimed. 'I'm Doña Halvillo, Señorita Juliena's *madre*. I didn't mean to intrude.' She stepped back and closed the door behind her. Her daughter had followed her into the house. 'Juliena,' she chided. 'You could have told me what had happened.'

'You didn't give me chance, Mama,' Juliena said. Her tone was reasonable but underneath her compliant demeanor mirth bubbled near the surface. 'Do you want some refreshment after your long journey?'

Doña Halvillo's gaze took in the house, plain but clean and well kept, and accepted the invitation. She felt as if she had little choice but to be civil and she smiled, pleased that her daughter showed no animosity towards her.

Juliena brought in a tray from the kitchen with cold lemonade and glasses. Doña Halvillo, travel-worn after the journey, took an appreciative sip. Refreshed, she quickly sought answers to her many questions.

'So, where do you reside, Juliena? After all it's a small residence when you consider the ranch has two extra women and a baby to accommodate.'

'I sleep in the master bedroom, Mama.'

The sip of lemonade emerged in a spray from the Doña's mouth as she experienced a fit of coughing. Juliena mischievously said nothing to quell her mama's hysteria, merely finding a handkerchief to offer to her.

'Do try another sip of lemonade,' she consoled.

'I don't think I could ever take another drink again.' Doña Halvillo wiped her mouth and brow theatrically. 'I knew your papa was wrong to send you to this heathen place.'

Juliena relented. 'Mama, the men sleep in the bunkhouse. They've given over the house to the women and the baby. I don't think a howling infant sits well with them.'

Doña Halvillo closed her eyes and sighed. On her face, relief replaced concern as she relaxed. 'Well, I'm pleased to hear it. I thought I'd never be able to find a suitable young man for you if the circumstances were, er, different.'

Juliena looked at her mother and expressed surprise. 'Mama, I have a marriage contract here,' she explained. 'I will marry Bart Gilson's nephew. Nothing has changed.'

Doña Halvillo sniffed as if the air suddenly had a bad smell to it. 'Nothing has changed?' she asked. 'What is all that outside? It's a land unfit for pigs, let alone sheep.'

Juliena sighed. Her mama was fixed in her views. She frowned to convey her hope that her papa wasn't so implacable. She refilled her mother's glass and poured herself a drink.

The atmosphere was tense. Juliena looked at the glass as if she wished it contained tequila.

CHAPTER
TWENTY-EIGHT

Charles Gilson surveyed the northern end of his land.

It was a complete mess.

Yet he savored the notion. 'His land.'

He liked the sound of it. He knew it couldn't officially be his until he'd married Juliena Halvillo. He shivered although it was never cold in Kansas, he thought, so perhaps it was the uncomfortable idea of being attached to a beautiful woman who felt no attraction to him. She hadn't said so but he couldn't see why she wanted to stay at the ranch. In his mind he pictured the fussy Doña Halvillo and decided he'd rather be anywhere than with her.

What an obligation Bart Gilson had put in his will!

All through his life his uncle had dogged him with a ridiculous name and now he pursued him after his death.

He shrugged his shoulders philosophically. Perhaps his uncle had given him a chance to settle down. Marriage to Juliena Halvillo wouldn't be a match made in heaven, but he reckoned if she was practical-minded enough to go through with it, then they'd both manage to make it work.

He recalled Doña Halvillo's predictable reaction to the oil on the land.

'Do you truly believe people will pay for this awful stuff?' she asked.

'It's called "black gold",' Don Halvillo answered. He tried to explain more about it but his wife's face fixed into an obstinate stare and she kicked at a piece of tar with the toe of her boot.

'Gold? I don't think I'll have a bracelet made of it,' she said.

She'd objected to the marriage. She hadn't wanted the ceremony to take place but Don Halvillo had interceded and, rarely, imposed his decision on his wife.

'The deal is done, was done with Bart Gilson. I am not one to go back on a contract. I will not dishonor a man even if he is dead. It will take place at the end of the week on Friday.' His tone implied he'd accept no objections. Even from Gilson.

'So soon?' Doña Halvillo and Juliena asked the question in unison.

'I wish to return home.' The Don stated his reason and refused to discuss it further.

She'd shaken her head as if despairing for her daughter's future. The Halvillos had decided to lodge at Fall River Hotel. The place was in Neodesha and suited their needs. Juliena went with them. Doña Halvillo had insisted that her daughter would not stay in the house of the man she was about to marry.

This discussion took place on Monday and they all had

barely five days to get ready. Now it was Thursday evening and Gilson didn't know whether he was ready yet. Of course, he'd got a clean pair of pants and shirt. He'd found a jacket, in Uncle Bart's cupboard, and a bright red bandanna to brighten up the dark clothes he wore. He'd even brushed his felt Stetson hat and polished his leather boots for the occasion. He'd confessed his misgivings in a rare moment of comradeship with Jack Edwards.

'Take it from me, son, no man is ever ready for his wedding,' Jack chortled. 'I had fifteen happy years before the good Lord took my wife. Maybe you'll be as lucky.'

Gilson clicked his tongue and his horse left off grazing and came up to him. The splashed-white paint pinto horse was a faithful, sturdy beast and they had an unbreakable bond between them. He'd bought it a couple of years ago and now man and horse were inseparable.

He looked up at the sky and wondered whether the following day would bring any relief in the heat. There'd been no rain, never was in Kansas, Jack told him, or at least not enough. In Wilson County the bushes looked for dogs. At other times the hot air and wind whipped up a tornado and tore everything in its path. Only time it felt cool was in January.

'Welcome to Kansas,' he'd said.

Gilson was so absorbed in viewing the land and trying to think things through that he didn't notice anyone approach until the rider was almost by his side.

Gilson's eyes widened as he recognized the visitor. The voice was from the past: thin, reedy, and sour. He hadn't seen him in ten years. The boy was a man. His broad upper body perched on wizened legs.

'I bet you didn't expect me to turn up.'

'I'm surprised, that's all, Garry Tucker.'

'Yes, you would be. You left me for dead.'

'That ain't true,' Gilson said. 'I ran for help.'

'You didn't hang around afterwards.'

Gilson hung his head. 'That's right. I took Ma's advice. She told me to leave. I shouldn't have.'

'I could've been dead.' Tucker continued speaking as if he'd not heard Gilson. 'They were gonna cut my leg off. But I begged the doc to leave it.' He pointed towards his kneecap. 'Sometimes I wish I'd taken his advice. It's like dragging a dead thing about.'

'If I can help you in any way I'll do it.' Guilt filled Gilson's voice. 'I owe you that at least.'

Tucker's eyes were dark and unreadable. If eyes were supposed to be windows of the soul, Gilson reckoned Tucker had lost his. He shook the thoughts away as if they were too fanciful for a man.

'I might have good oil in this land. I'll need someone to help me run the place. I'll offer you the job for a share in the profits. I know you got a good memory.'

They both knew he alluded to the argument that had sparked the fight. Tucker and Gilson had never been friends; Tucker was a bully. When he couldn't beat you with his fists he'd use words.

Garry Tucker nodded. 'Yes, Mr Charles Wallace Leopold Augustine Gabriel Bartholomew Gilson. My memory is as good as it ever was. You were such a baby . . . squawking 'cause I called you names. Your own names.'

'I admit I was cussed and muley,' Gilson agreed.

He recalled the anger – it had caused a fight. He was

cleaning his gun and in the struggle between them it went off.

Tucker pulled himself upright in his saddle. He had to use the horn to sit straight.

'I don't want your job, your profits.' He spat out the words and the spittle dribbled over his lips. 'I want you to feel what it's like to be useless. Unemployable. Less than a man.'

Gilson lifted his hand away from his gun. 'I won't fight. Offer stands. Come back with me to the ranch.'

He pulled the reins, pressed his thighs against his horse as a signal for it to turn.

'Don't turn away from me.'

Garry Tucker, Gilson saw, had a gun in his hands. His arms had the strength his legs did not.

Gilson shook his head. 'I don't want to fight. It caused enough trouble last time.'

CHAPTER TWENTY-NINE

Gilson opened his eyes.

It was dark.

He tried to sit up. He couldn't move other than to lift his head but that didn't get him very far. He relaxed his body and tried to figure out what had happened. It felt as if his head had been split open with an axe. He recalled nothing after the moment he'd turned to ride away from Garry Tucker.

There was a loud boom, then nothing.

A short, sharp laugh interrupted his muse. His eyes got used to the initial darkness although it was very hazy. He could make out the shadowy shape of Garry Tucker.

'What's happened ?' he asked. 'What do you want?'

'You're so full of questions,' Tucker said. 'You wouldn't fight me 'cause I'm a cripple but I'm gonna even things up. I shot a bit of your brain out. Didn't want to do that 'cause I want you to feel all the pain I've suffered all these years. An' it's no use calling out for help 'cause we're deep down in the ground. Your ma can't help you now.'

Gilson experienced the feeling of being both hot and cold. His blood pounded around his body and the sweat turned to ice as his hopeless position became clear. His head pounded where the bullet had creased him. He looked at his surroundings. A small lamp lit up what seemed to be a cave.

'Where am I?'

'Some sort of oil shaft. Couldn't have wished to find a better place. You can holler all you want. No one will hear you.'

Gilson felt ropes at his wrists and ankles bound to stakes pushed into the earth. He pulled frantically against his restraints.

'Don't bother. I've had plenty of time to practice knots. In fact, I couldn't walk for nigh-on twelve months. It took a long time to stand up again and even longer to take a step.' Tucker shifted uncomfortably on his crutch, grimaced and then a smile lit up his face. 'For years I thought about what I'd do if we ever met up. I've been here a while watching you while you been out cold. Let me tell you it's been a real pleasure going over those thoughts again.'

'Folks will be out looking for me,' Gilson said.

The threat sounded empty even to his ears. Who would bother about a gunslinger? Don Halvillo and Jack Edwards would assume he'd decided to drift off again. Juliena would believe he'd run away from marriage and Doña Halvillo would be overjoyed that he wasn't around to wed her beloved daughter. Don Halvillo might decide to invest in oil and Lou Wainwright would get a headache about the legality of it all. If they decided to search for him, who would think to look down the shaft of a deserted old oil well?

'I've heard stories about you and I'd say you've been nowhere long enough to put down roots. I only got to know you were here 'cause the marshal wanted a reason to lock you up. In fact I'd go as far as to say no one gives a cuss about you.'

Tucker's manic laughter bounced off the walls and Gilson felt the urge to laugh with him. He swallowed and suppressed it. His laughter would sound crazier to his ears than Tucker's rattle.

Every word rang true to Gilson. It hit home harder than a bullet. He closed his eyes and the energy seeped out of him. He was helpless and without hope. A sharp pain in his side made start and cry out. He looked up; Tucker had a stick in his hand with a spike at the end. He lifted it up to show Gilson.

'How'd you like my little toy?' he said. 'Made with you in mind. Now you keep those eyes open. I want you to see what's happening to you.'

'If you hate me so much why didn't you set the law after me? No one would've believed me. I'd have gone to jail.'

Tucker shifted his stance again, as if it hurt to stay in the same position for long on his withered leg.

'I did regret it at first, then I began thinking that one day I'd get you. You dang well ran around too much an' I thought I'd never catch up with you. Your ma, bless her heart, took pity on me an' she told me what you were up to and all.' He sighed and paused in what seemed to be a well-rehearsed speech. 'Your ma regretted encouraging you to run away.' Gilson saw Tucker's face pull into a wicked grin. 'An' I think she took me under her wing as if I was a son, or something. I would say she was the proudest hen in the coop regards me.' He bent towards Gilson as if to make sure he didn't miss his next words. 'We got very close.'

'What you saying?'

Tucker's insult to his ma filled Gilson with both rage and fresh energy. He pulled violently against the ropes. They cut into his flesh but held him tight.

'You're gonna have to suffer a lot of things before you go. Words will be the least of your pain, although perhaps for you words are your undoing. I'll tell you more stories about your ma. Later.'

Tucker jabbed the spike into Gilson again and again and again until he leant against a wall, exhausted by his actions.

Blood spurted from the wounds and Gilson became aware he lay in a pool of liquid. He felt sick. He lifted his head slightly and tried to see what had happened. He twitched his nose and touched the ground. It was sticky as he rubbed it between his fingers.

His face filled with hope. Although the ropes were secure it might be possible to work the posts loose. The ground wasn't as hard as he and, perhaps Tucker, had anticipated. Gilson pulled at the posts to test his theory. Disappointingly, though, they were stuck fast in the ground.

As if irritated by Gilson's struggles, Tucker used the stick to hit at Gilson's arm. It wasn't a good hit; at least not for Tucker. The stick smashed down on the post and he almost fell. If Tucker had hit him, Gilson reckoned he'd have ended up with a broken wrist. Tucker pitched forward and Gilson automatically twisted to avoid him. The post Tucker hit had moved slightly. He looked towards Tucker and stopped wondering how he could incapacitate the man. He saw Tucker grab his crutch to stay upright. His gait was sluggish and awkward. Once off his feet he'd be as helpless as a beetle on his back.

The challenge would be to put him down and keep him down. Gilson knew he couldn't count on Tucker missing him every time but he reckoned if he struggled the posts might get an extra bash to loosen them and take Tucker off his feet.

It would equal the odds.

CHAPTER THIRTY

'What's it like to be no good to anyone?'

Gilson attempted to bait Tucker into anger. He couldn't use his physical strength so like Tucker he used words against him. He wanted to make him hit the post again. However, Tucker seemed to know the post had become loose and was wary now.

He stabbed him with the spike instead but not very hard.

'Don't want to end it too quick,' he joked. 'I can use both my crutch and this stick like they were extensions of my arms.'

There wasn't much space in the disused shaft. Tucker had avoided Gilson with his feet although he guessed that had he been able Tucker would've trodden all over him. Gilson continued to pull his wrist. He focused on the loose post.

Tucker growled.

'Leave it alone.'

His stick followed through with his order and although it caught Gilson's wrist it banged into the post again. The

141

shock raced through his body and he bit his lips to stop crying out in pain. He prayed his bones weren't broken but it felt as if they were shattered into pulp. He continued to pull as he became insensible to the pain.

Gilson shut his eyes for a brief moment and visualized his hand free. Then he'd be able to sit up, fight back. He'd still be tied at the ankles but it would give him the chance to pull his opponent down. They'd be equal, almost, and Gilson would have a chance of leaving this hell.

It suddenly occurred to him; his horse was a marker at the top of the shaft. He looked towards Tucker. He laughed out loud.

'You made a mistake, Tucker,' he said.

'What?' Tucker frowned.

'My horse,' he said.

The man seemed unperturbed. 'There ain't no horse out there,' he said. Gilson's eyebrows rose, puzzled. 'I tied my horse up some distance away where it won't be noticed. I shot yours.'

Tucker stated it in such a matter-of-fact way that Gilson didn't react immediately. He thought he'd misheard. Tucker made sure he understood.

'I had to consider the slim chance that someone might look around for you. So I made sure your horse wasn't hanging around. I brought it into this shaft.' Gilson looked all around. 'Oh, this place is deep. I led it to the edge and when I put a bullet in it, it toppled towards the bottom of the shaft. If you could move you'd see its carcass.'

Gilson roared with fury.

'Sorry. Did you like that horse? I bet you called it all

142

sorts of fancy names. How about "Squash"? That'd suit it now.'

The more he listened to Garry Tucker the more he believed that the shattered knee was the least of the man's problems. He sounded as if he'd been shot in the head and lost part of his brain rather than his kneecap. Bile threatened to spew from his mouth as his stomach reeled.

He pulled against his fixtures. He extended his fingers, then clenched as he tried to escape. Tucker laughed but he didn't have the last laugh. Gilson's outstretched hand caught Tucker's crutch and his misery turned to triumph. He held his future in his palm and it didn't include a death in a cold, dark place.

Tucker tried to pull free, stabbing Gilson as he did so, but adrenaline coursed through Gilson's veins and he seemed immune from anything but the fight for survival. Tucker flailed wildly as he tried to regain his stance.

He'd underestimated Gilson. To his way of thinking, Gilson was a ma's boy and under duress he'd crack. He became aware that the boy was a man who had toughened up. His ma broke the apron strings when she'd told him to run. Now he knew the trail of dead bodies should've warned him he was up against a man-killer.

Tucker tried to hit Gilson's arm, his grip vice-like as he rained blows down on the body staked out on the ground. He missed frequently. The pressure on his injured leg began to wear him down.

'Let go,' Tucker shouted.

He saw a sneer on Gilson's face. It was the look of a man in ascension. He pulled violently to escape. And fell. Now he was at Gilson's level. He retched and coffee, grits and beans erupted from his stomach, ran down his shirt, and dribbled towards the back of his neck. Weakly, Tucker lifted his head, then let it fall back into the vomit.

Gilson let go of Tucker's ankle once the man had fallen and pulled desperately on the stake. It came out. He sat up; although still hampered by the other bonds he felt that now he had a fighting chance. His fingers felt as if they were broken but he ignored the pain. Tucker lay on the ground and Gilson reckoned he had but a short space of time to get free. He didn't know whether Tucker had a gun but he didn't want to find out when he was still in this position.

As luck would have it the spiked stick had fallen by his side and he pulled it towards him. On examination it was a simple weapon, a knife blade bound onto the end of a stick, but it was just the thing to help him get free. He held the stick near to the blade and sawed the rope from his other wrist. The pain slowed the action until he heard Tucker moan and despite his hand he worked harder. The rope sprang away and he now had two hands free. He sat up and bent towards his feet.

Gilson looked behind him; he saw Tucker try to get up.

The one on his feet first would win the fight.

CHAPTER THIRTY-ONE

'I don't believe he's gone!'

Juliena stamped her foot to emphasize her words. Her mama shrugged her shoulders dispassionately.

'Well, he's not here.' She looked as if she might add a salty comment, but refrained and tried to comfort her daughter. 'Sometimes things are for the best.' Then Doña Halvillo placed her arm around her daughter. The young woman sat next to her mother and put her head on her shoulder.

'It's your best,' Juliena said.

'Don't fret,' she said. 'Come home with us and we'll look after you. Everything will be as it used to be.'

Juliena clasped her mother's hand. 'Things don't go back to how they used to be,' she said. 'If he's gone . . . well, he's gone. I will remain here. I've made this place my home for the past couple of years. I'm happy and I see no reason to leave.'

'What about marriage, family—'

Juliena interrupted her. 'Sometimes things happen . . . and you have to go along with it. I mean, look how Mrs Bonde has settled in Neodesha with Mrs Mattern. Who would've thought they'd both set up as *modistas*?'

Doña Halvillo sniffed at the idea of 'trade' but had to concede that being a seamstress was respectable.

Juliena got up and walked towards the door. 'However, Mama, I haven't given up yet. Mrs Mattern and Mrs Bonde have finished my wedding dress. I don't want it to hang, as food for moths, in a wardrobe.' Doña Halvillo opened her mouth to speak but Juliena brought her finger to her own lips to shush her. 'Maybe another beau will come along, Mama, but I don't believe Chaz Gilson has gone. I'm going to ride out and see whether something has happened.'

The Doña said nothing to dissuade her daughter. It was clear to her from the look of determination on her face; Juliena wasn't a woman to give up easily.

Juliena saddled her sorrel horse and mounted it. She'd plaited her long brunette locks, secured them in a snood at the back of her head, and pushed them under her hat. She was an experienced horsewoman who liked to ride with the wind pulling at her hair but today she needed to look composed as if to show the world that she wasn't a distressed damsel who'd been ditched at the altar. She needed to ride out whether she found Chaz Gilson or not.

The hot wind with its granules of sand stung her face. She didn't mind in fact; it concentrated the pain away from her heart and put the ache in a different place. She blamed it for causing the stinging tears in her eyes and blamed her headache on the horse's pounding hoofs. The

146

stink of oil filled her nostrils and she hated it even more than she had before.

'Damn black stuff has taken the grass from the sheep. It's taken my dowry.'

She shouted as the horse galloped. There was no one to hear her curse. She didn't look to see how far she'd come until the scenery changed. Ahead she spotted a few dogies at a small pool. They'd soon be rounded up and branded: Mavericks no more.

As she slowed her horse to a canter and then a halt, Juliena dismounted. The animal was exercised but thirsty. They both liked to get away from everything. She used her hat as a scoop and took a drink. She had a water bottle but the lake sparkled invitingly as if with diamonds on the aqua-blue surface in the sunshine.

Juliena secured her horse to allow it to graze and sat and looked across the water. It wasn't immediately obvious but in amongst the cattle were a couple of horses. They were unsaddled but weren't wild, she surmised as she watched. The paint horse looked familiar. It had a dark coat but its legs and head had been dipped in white paint apart from its dark mane. The horse turned and looked towards her before its head went down again to graze. It was then she noticed a dark star on its forehead. So distinctive she couldn't believe she'd missed it.

She whistled. Just as she'd heard Chaz do when he wanted his horse. The animal looked up and she whistled again. Cautiously, it moved towards her, sniffing the air as it did so, and Juliena thought it would turn and run away. The horse held its head high and snorted with a flutter of its nostrils. Juliena didn't move; she didn't want to startle it. Then it started to nicker and gradually moved towards her. When it got closer she patted its neck and whispered to it.

'Where is your master?' The neigh came again. It held its head up and started to squeal. 'Easy, easy,' Juliena said. The horse reacted to her words and it nickered again, pushing its head against her. 'Let's get you back to the ranch,' she said. Then she looked round. 'Where are your saddle and reins? And who does that other horse belong to?'

There were too many unanswered questions. She decided to return home and get some men to look for Chaz. He hadn't left. No man would forsake his horse – unless he was dead. The chill thought mobilized her into action.

Juliena manipulated the lariat into a rope bridle, talking soothingly to the horse. She kept hold of the reins as she remounted her own horse and took the horses at a slow pace. If she'd missed a horse, she reasoned, what else had she not seen?

The answer was provided before the sun dipped down and disappeared below the horizon.

Poorly camouflaged tack and a couple of saddles plus bags were hidden at the base of a cottonwood tree. A concerned look on her face, she dismounted and investigated. His fancy saddle was there so it definitely meant Chaz Gilson's disappearance wasn't voluntarily. She took the rope bridle off his horse and slapped its rump.

'Go home,' she shouted.

The horse reared up slightly in surprise but then, almost as if it knew what was wanted, galloped off in the direction of the ranch. She hoped the folks back at the ranch would work out Chaz was in trouble. She watched the horse's dust trail and then went to look for him.

If it occurred to her that she might be in trouble as well, the resolute expression on her face dismissed it as a fleeting thought.

She recalled seeing an old oil shaft earlier. It was right ahead of her. Juliena instinctively decided that it was a good place to hide. She tethered the horse's reins with a stone. It wasn't very secure but the horse had no reason to bolt. Fortunately, Juliena had dressed for a workday at the ranch rather than in her full riding costume. Her old leather vest worn over a cotton shirt, which tucked neatly into a pair of pants, wouldn't hamper her exploration. She hesitated for a moment and then decided to take a weapon with her. She pushed her Remington .44 pistol into the waistband of her pants, felt the warmth of its walnut grip against her, and then pulled her neckerchief over her face. She was ready to investigate.

The shaft, long out of use, stood derelict at the boundary of Gilson land. She'd asked Bart Gilson about it when she'd first come to live on the ranch and he'd told her it was a folly. She recalled not having any idea what a folly was and merely looked wise and knowing. It was later that Jack Edwards told her they'd tried to find oil.

'Bart regretted wasting money on the hole. He used a natural shaft that was already there and tried to dig down. Evidently, there's oil in the North, but no one has found anything here, apart from bits of black stuff that the Indians gather up and exchange as a remedy for every ailment going.' Edwards had laughed. 'Don't be tempted to taste the stuff, though,' he said. 'I reckon it would give you more ailments than it ever cured.'

She had no expectation of finding anything but stepped over the ground cautiously with her soft leather boots to avoid making a sound. If anything was amiss then she had to be careful not to warn anyone that she was around. She waited by the entrance to the shaft and listened. She thought she heard the sound of men's voices. Low, angry growls.

Juliena reckoned she had two courses of action.

She could turn round, head back and wait for help to arrive. That would be sensible. More risky and immediate was to continue on her present course.

It took no time at all to decide. As far as she was concerned Chaz Gilson was in a lot of trouble. Juliena, convinced she could face any situation, headed into the mouth of the shaft.

CHAPTER THIRTY-TWO

Tucker watched helplessly as Gilson grabbed hold of the knife he'd so carefully bound to the stick.

He roared. 'I'll kill you, Gilson. You see if I don't.'

'Did you think you could outwit me, Tucker? You couldn't teach a hen to cluck,' he said.

Gilson's expression was distorted by malevolence and anger.

He recalled conversations with his ma as he tried to explain why he had to fight Garry Tucker: 'I'm sick of the name-calling. It's worse than the bruises he gives me.'

'Now, I don't want you to fight, Charles,' his ma harangued him. 'We believe the Lord asks us to turn the other cheek.'

He couldn't hide the blackened eyes, split lips and torn clothes from her. He challenged her beliefs. 'Don't the Bible say an eye for an eye and a tooth for a tooth?'

'That's enough, Charles. You should be proud of the

name you got when you were baptized.'

'God gave me that name, then? I recall it was Uncle Bart who—'

He'd never got to finish the sentence. His ma believed that children should respect their elders and ended the discussion with a hickory stick. It taught him to hold his tongue. It never stopped him hating Garry Tucker. It wasn't only constant name-calling; it was the punches, and the fact he wasn't allowed to hit him back, not without suffering an extra hiding.

Now Tucker was at his mercy. Gilson watched as the man flailed around as he tried to get up.

Gallons of self-pity oozed out. 'You made me like this,' he moaned.

'Brought it on yourself,' Gilson answered. 'Not content with the name-calling an' all, you wanted my things.' The gun was his pa's. One of the few possessions he owned to remember him by. 'You tried to take my gun. It went off. It could've been either of us who got hurt.'

Gilson had been only six when his pa left to find gold in California. In his dreams he figured his pa had given him the gun as defense. Ma was overprotective and so anxious, well, it was like she didn't want him to grow up. He knew it didn't excuse the fact that when he should've acted like a man he'd taken the easy option and run.

Slowly he hauled his body upright but nearly fell as his legs wobbled beneath him. He shook them to rid the tingling sensation.

He kept his gaze on Tucker, who'd crawled over to a wood support. Spittle bubbled over Tucker's lips like a madman in a fit as he too struggled to stand.

'You had more than me, always had,' Tucker said. 'The marshal said you've even got this goddamn ranch.'

'I had no pa,' Gilson said. 'He left to look for gold an' never came back. Ma had to work hard.'

He went quiet. Perhaps he'd judged his ma too hard. He hadn't put in half the work he should've, he reckoned. A picture of his ma flashed through his mind. She must be near fifty; time to sit in a rocker on the porch and have an easy time at the end of her days. He vowed to send for her if he ever got out of this fix.

Tucker was on his feet, propped up by his crutch.

'Well, I had both a ma and pa,' Tucker said. 'Only they sat an' drunk Hoochino and let the homestead go to ruin.'

'So that was my fault?'

'Don't suppose it was, but that don't matter none; you made things worse. My pa wanted to know why I wasn't as useful as you. I hated you.' Tucker looked like a man who'd come to the end of the road. 'You gonna kill me? You've killed everyone else who upset you.'

His eyes drooped pathetically and he sounded like a puppy howling to Gilson. He couldn't murder a man he'd already maimed.

'Let's call it evens,' Gilson said. Blood trickled down his shirt and pants and he swayed slightly. 'You get out of this place and I won't kill you or get the law after you.'

'The law? I did nothing.' He stood more firmly in his upright stance. His attitude seemed defiant now. As if Gilson's refusal to take revenge made him weak. He continued to goad him even though he knew the risks. 'At least, I didn't do what I came here to do.'

Gilson raised his hand and scratched his head. He

looked towards heaven and sighed. 'What does it take to get you to go?'

Gilson made a mistake; he'd momentarily moved his gaze from Tucker. Now he looked down the barrel of a gun. There were several feet between them but the gun had shortened the gulf.

'I want you dead. That's what it takes.'

'Now look, Tucker, you've had your fun. I'm as full of holes from that damn spike as a miner's sieve. I ain't got a crippled knee but I'm dang not running anywhere soon. Let's call it quits.'

'I ain't calling quits until you're dead.'

'You'll get hung for murder. Your lame legs will dance around like any other man's with a hemp necktie round you.'

'No one will find you here.'

Gilson sensed Tucker, consumed with hatred, wasn't going to let him leave the shaft alive. He figured Garry Tucker wouldn't be able to salvage his pride until he stood over his dead body.

Of all the situations Gilson had been in over the years, he hadn't envisioned his body left to rot in the depths of the earth. He could've chosen differently: slower on the draw in a gunfight; thrown out of a bar onto the street and run over by a carriage; got shot up by a jealous lover – if he had the time he could've thought up a hundred different ends. Time was one thing he was short of. He scanned around, desperately looking for a way to defeat Tucker.

On an even scale Gilson knew he was faster than his opponent even though the blood loss made him weak.

He wasn't faster than a bullet.
A bullet would win the fight.

CHAPTER THIRTY-THREE

It was silent in the old underground shaft.

Juliena trod softly on the wet soil. The earth seemed to suck at her boots and she bent down to brush off a piece of it with her gloved hand. It was sticky. Tar-like. So, Bart's dreams weren't all ballyhoo, she thought; he'd merely given up too soon. If there was oil near the stream and here, too, then the whole of the land could contain the black gold.

She frowned. Now it was easy to understand Alden's interest in the Gilson Ranch. It was probably the reason for Bart Gilson's death.

Juliena continued further into the shaft. There was light to see by, which was strange as she anticipated the deeper she went the darker it would become. She didn't call out, until she knew what she faced. She stepped carefully although she had to bite back a cry of alarm when one foot found nothing beneath it. Furiously she fought to keep her balance but as she pulled back she ended up in the black mud. The shaft evidently sloped sharply so she felt around the edge for a way to the bottom.

Chaz would be there. He was a man who needed help. She was wary, suspicious, and on her guard. The slope was gentle to the left of her, almost a path into the bowels of the earth. Juliena, without another thought for her own safety, trekked down until she reached a sight that made her stomach lurch with surprise and horror.

Gilson saw a movement behind Tucker. He didn't know whether it was an accomplice or whether help had arrived. He couldn't figure it out. He gave no indication that he'd seen anything.

He immediately dismissed the notion that Tucker had a friend in tow. Like him he'd been a loner. Tucker never had any friends, when he thought about it. He was a bully whose few companions feared him. That was until he got his gammy leg. Then he'd heard how the bully had become the bullied.

So who was there? He couldn't risk bringing attention to the other person. It could be an animal, he supposed, but as the unpleasant smell of oil surfaced to his consciousness again he couldn't think of anything that would want to take refuge down here.

'You've gone quiet. You must be contemplating your demise, Charles Wallace Leopold Augustine Gabriel Bartholomew Gilson. I'd put up a headstone but I don't think I'd have room to carve your name!'

'No. He's looking at me.' Juliena took in the situation, stepped right up to the man with the gun and pushed a gun into his neck. 'Drop the weapon or I'll shoot you full of lead.'

Tucker froze. He did as he was told and let the gun fall.

'Juliena,' Gilson said.

It wasn't who he expected at all.

'Yes. I had to come and find you. Everyone reckons you rode off at full spit to avoid your wedding vows. Can't have you embarrassing a lady like that,' she answered.

The pair were distracted for a moment. Tucker took his chance. He struck out with his elbow and caught Juliena under the ribs. The breath left her body and, winded, she collapsed on the floor.

'I'll get you if she's come to any harm,' Gilson shouted.

He moved forward but Tucker blocked his way. Gilson didn't expect him to fight and when Tucker caught him with a blow to his nose and cheek he reeled back, slipped on the oil and went down. Tucker held on to the post and used his crutch to pull his gun towards him. He picked it up.

'I wasn't going to give you a quick end,' Tucker said. His face screwed up into something resembling a smile, but not quite. 'I can still riddle you with a few bullets before the final one.'

He aimed the gun at Gilson's knee. The gun clicked.

'Darn it.' Tucker checked his gun. 'The thing has gummed up in this black stuff.' His gaze darted around and he saw the gun that had fallen from Juliena's hand. 'This'll do the trick.'

Gilson rolled away from the line of fire. He knew he presented such a large target he was going to be hit somewhere but he tried to protect his vitals. He saw Tucker lift the gun, aim, and fire. The shot went wild as a knife went through the back of his neck. He jumped about like a puppet on a string.

Juliena stood behind him with the stick that had the blade secured to it. She twisted the blade.

'He's dancing with the Devil now,' she said.

She let the stick drop and Gilson, now on his feet, went to her side.

'Let's get outta here,' he said.

'Yes, Mr Charles Wallace Leopold Augustine Gabriel Bartholomew Gilson, you got a wedding to attend.' Her teeth showed like pearls between red lips. 'You don't laugh at my names?'

'What's that?'

'Juliena Vittoria Adelina Silvia Pilar Halvillo.'

'If we have any little shavers, we'll call them plain Jane or John,' Chaz Gilson said.